MORE STORIES FOR AROUND

T

by

No

PUBLI

CAMP
8107 B
LAUR

by RAY HARRIOT

Dedicated to youth leaders everywhere who have taken the time and energy to captivate and mold the minds of our young people. The future is in your hands.

ISBN 0-9617653-1-3

TABLE OF CONTENTS

MORE SERIOUS STORIES

INTRODUCTION

Is there any better way to end a fun-filled weekend of camping than to sit around a campfire with your friends and fellow campers... enjoying some songs and skits... and climaxing it all with a story... just as darkness besets the campfire area and the coals begin to give off an eerie glow? I think not. Campfires and related activities have always been high on campers' lists of favorite things — but good campfires, like good campouts, don't come without prior planning.

Unfortunately, my thirty years experience as a youth leader showed that there was a lack of material for the kinds of stories that boys and girls wanted to hear. For the most part children want to be scared, yet remain assured that it is still safe to be out-of-doors. This is particularly true with younger children. Older children have a much easier time understanding that it's just a story... and they don't take the emotions back to their tent with them.

Because of that, I resorted to making-up my own stories. I used ideas from other Scouters, punch lines from jokes that my Scouts told along the trail, and historical facts about the camping areas we frequented to come up with several short stories that could easily be told around a campfire. I found that these stories were easily adaptable; that is they could be readily modified to fit various situations. I had stories for cabin campouts, lake campouts, hiking trips... stories about pirates, Indians, vampires, and more. They went over so well that my Scouts encouraged me to put them down on paper which I did in my first book ***Stories for Around the Campfire***. Now ***Stories for Around the Campfire*** has been selling for over ten years... and those stories have entertained thousands of children from coast to coast... so the time was right for some new ones.

More Stories for Around the Campfire contains twenty-three additional short stories for telling around the campfire... and like the first book you will find stories for all ages. The stories toward the front of the book are scary to a point, but climax with a punch line that sort of says "GOTCHA". These are more suitable for younger children though older children and adults have been HAD as well. The stories toward the back are scarier and should be reserved for older children. Please feel free to modify them as you see fit — that's all part of the art of storytelling.

For the novice storyteller, I have again included a short tutorial on how to effectively tell stories. There's more to it than just the words. You need to set the stage. You need to be prepared..

So it's time to sit back, read the stories... then put the book back on the shelf and entertain.

Hope you enjoy.

TELLING THE STORY

The following procedures should be considered before telling a story at a campfire. Please read them thoroughly. They are your guide to years of successful campfire stories.

SELECTING THE STORY

There are many factors that the storyteller must consider when choosing a story to tell to a group of children. The first factor is the age of the group. Different age groups will react differently to various types of stories. For example, children of all age groups should enjoy the humorous stories in the beginning of this book, whereas some stories toward the back may be too serious for a young group to understand. Some stories that would not scare older children may make younger children uneasy. Age also affects the attention span. Older children have a longer attention span, though not much longer, than younger children.

This leads to the next factor, which is the length of the story. Campfire stories should be kept short. A good story should last no longer than twenty minutes. This is particularly true for those stories that are told at a campfire culminating a long day's activities. Often the storyteller will find it necessary to condense the story to fit within these limits. Do it! It will make it easier on both you and your audience. Remember, with campfire stories shorter is usually better. All the stories in this book are easily told within these time limits.

Another factor to consider is the question, "What do you want to accomplish with the story?" Some stories are told strictly for fun while others may contain a moral or message. A campfire story is sometimes a good tool to get a point across to a young group. You'll find most of the stories in this book to be the "FUN" kind.

Finally, matching the theme or location of the story to that of the campfire will make the story more effective. A Civil War story while camping at Gettysburg would be better received than one about pirates, though the latter would be a hit at an ocean campout. Children prefer stories they can relate to their personal experiences or environment.

Keep the above in mind when choosing your story, and your storytelling will be on the trail to success.

GETTING FAMILIAR

Any storyteller must be thoroughly familiar with the story to be told. The story should be read repeatedly until all the facts are straight in your mind. Know the main characters and major events of the story, and the order in which they occur. Delete minor events if you are afraid the story cannot be told in fifteen to twenty minutes. Run over the story several times in your mind. Make sure it flows smoothly. This sounds like work, and it is, but the results are well worth it. If the storyteller appears uncertain of the facts, the audience will sense it, and the whole story will lose credibility. At all cost, avoid reading the story from a book. The children can do that themselves.

Use the Scout Motto — "BE PREPARED." Campfires are not normally impromptu events. If you know there will be a campfire, come prepared with a story. After awhile your library of campfire stories will grow, and it will take less and less time to get prepared.

CHANGING THE STORY

It is the storyteller's right to change the story to suit the location or mood of a campfire to enhance the story's effect — and I highly recommend it. The names of rivers, lakes, and such can all be changed. Also, changing the names and ages of the main characters in the story can have some interesting effects. If the star of the story is an eleven year old, blond boy, named Jimmy, and everyone knows there happens to be such a boy in the audience, there are all sorts of possibilities. Boys' names can be changed to girls' names for a female group. Any time the storyteller can use things to relate to the audience — familiar names, troop numbers, places, experiences, etc. — the chances of maintaining interest and everyone enjoying themselves is increased.

ESTABLISHING THE SETTING

Sometimes the setting of the campfire itself can greatly affect the success of a campfire story. Is the fire situated so that everyone can hear the storyteller? Children who can't hear may become disruptive. How is the fire? Generally, most stories are more appropriate at the end of a campfire when the coals are hot and glowing, giving an eerie effect. Make sure it is quiet! Do not allow the actions of some children to ruin the story for others.

Avoid distractions such as flashlights. Listeners should be instructed that no flashlight should be turned on during the story.

Finally, make sure the audience has something to focus on during the story. Often the hot coals are sufficient. Other times, I have used a flashlight with a red lens that I hold to my chin as I talk. By focusing their eyes on some object, the children tend to let their minds cast themselves into the story.

DELIVERY

Always let the audience know that you expect complete silence and attention during the story. Once this is established, a slight pause when noise is heard will normally return the calm. Don't talk in a monotone. Be involved in your story. Use hand movements, feet movements, or a quick turn of the head to add to the story. Remember, you are the artist and you are painting a picture for your audience. Provide enough description of your main characters and story location for your audience to visualize them. The need for this is lessened if you tailor the story to the area surrounding the campfire. Be careful not to be too descriptive as you only have twenty minutes. Allow the children some room to use their imagination.

Many stories are more effective if told in the first person as if you, the storyteller, were part of the story. Phrases such as "boys like you" or "with dark brown hair like Joey" will interject your audience into the story.

Be sure you cover all things that happen, who they happen to, and where and when they happen. Lead up to the conclusion. With experience, you will be able to sense if you have the audience where you want them.

PITFALLS TO AVOID

1. Do not use stories that contain material that may be offensive to any member of your audience.

2. Try not to use characters with similar names. They will be hard for you and your audience to remember and keep straight.

3. Avoid too much coincidence. Stories that have too much coincidence lose credibility.

4. Don't lose control of the group. Disruptive behavior, such as talking or flashlights, should be dealt with immediately.

5. Telling a story at all costs. One must recognize that there are times when a campfire will not be successful regardless of how good it is or how well it is told. Examples are if the listeners are extremely cold or wet.

ARNOLD

This is the story about Arnold, a very courageous boy, and how Scouting changed his life.

It all started when Arnold, the only son of Joe and Mary Wilson, was born under difficult circumstances. You see, Mary was seven months pregnant when she was involved in a serious automobile accident and had to be rushed to the hospital because of her injuries. Doctors fought long and hard to save her life and that of her unborn son. The baby had to be delivered two months early.

Both Mary and Arnold were in the operating room when Joe arrived at the hospital and that's when the doctor's gave him the news. Despite the seriousness of Mary's injuries, they were able to stabilize her and she'd survive... but the baby had to be delivered early... and it had not yet fully developed... and...

Mr. Wilson could see that the doctor was very hesitant. "Is he dead?" he asked.

"No, but... he has no arms... and he has no legs... and no body. He's only a head. Your son is nothing but a head! However, he appears to be holding on."

Mr. Wilson sat down and thanked God. Then he rushed to his wife's bedside to comfort her.

The next few weeks were critical to the recovery of both Mary and baby Arnold. Mary gained her strength quickly and visited Arnold at the hospital every day without fail. She blamed herself for the accident and Arnold's condition. Often she would stand there and look at Arnold while he was sleeping... those cute eyes... that cute nose... those cute ears... that cute mouth... and that cute bald head. She prayed that if God would help him survive that she would cherish him and love him despite his condition.

It was a miracle. Every day Arnold gained strength. Within weeks he went from a tomato-sized head to a melon-sized head. Soon he was ready to leave the hospital. At long last, Joe and Mary took him home.

Despite his disability, Arnold had quite a personality and was readily accepted into the family. And Mary, she kept her promise and loved and cherished him. Both Mary and Joe tried to raise him as best they could, but it wasn't always easy. They had to learn to adapt. For example, whereas most babies learn to crawl... and then to walk... Arnold just rolled. It was amazing how well Mary and Joe dealt with this situation. "Look on the bright side," Mary would always say, "we don't have to deal with messy diapers."

Medical people really didn't believe that Arnold would live very long. But by the age of two, Arnold was talking. He could also hear and think like a normal person. It must have been his attitude and disposition, plus the exceptional care and attention he got from his parents, that enabled him to prove those doctors wrong. It wasn't easy being a *head* but Arnold made the best of it. He was just thankful to be alive.

As part of her daily routine, Mary would t Arnold and place him in a half-rounded, bowl-like pedestal in the large bay window in the front of the house so that he could get some sunshine and look out at the world around him. Over the years this became Arnold's favorite time of day. He loved to look at the trees, the birds... see the changing of the seasons. But most of all he loved to look at the children playing in the park playground across the street. It always looked like they were having so much fun. Arnold knew, however, that he could not do those things. After all, he was just a *head*.

Then one day Jason Eaton was walking by Arnold's house on his way home from school. All of a sudden he felt this strange sensation. You know... like somebody was watching him. He stopped and looked around but didn't see anyone. He quickly ran home.

Of course, Arnold had been watching Jason all of the time... just like he had every day since school had started. Arnold watched all of the children that passed by his window perch or played in the playground across the street. I mean... what else was there for a *head* to do? He had plenty of time to look at them and analyze their traits. And he had noticed something different about Jason. He was always friendly to the other children. He never teased them or called them names. Jason wasn't one of the bullies. Tomorrow he'd stare harder.

The next day as Jason was returning home from school, he again had this strange sensation while passing Arnold's house. Again he stopped and looked around. That's when he saw Arnold, perched in his pedestal-bowl, in the Wilson window.

Arnold winked... and Jason smiled.

"You know," Jason thought, "I've passed this house every day for months and never noticed that boy in the window." Jason waved and then ran home.

Every day for the next week Jason never passed the Wilson house without waving to Arnold in the window... a wave which Arnold always acknowledged with a big wink. Then one day, on his way home from school, Jason gathered the nerve to knock on the Wilson door.

"Can I come in and play with your son?" he asked when Mary answered the door. She was floored. Nobody had ever asked to play with Arnold before. She didn't know what to say.

"Yes! Yes! Yes!" came the screams from the big bay window. And from that day on Jason and Arnold became the best of friends.

Jason would always stop by to talk and play after school... and Mary strongly encouraged it. Never before had Arnold been so happy. Never before had another boy showed so much caring — so Mary was not surprised to learn that Jason was a Boy Scout. She often overheard him telling Arnold about his Scouting adventures... the troop meetings, the campouts, and other activities... and she could see that Jason exemplified all of the good things she had always heard about Boy Scouts.

It wasn't long before Jason and Arnold were doing other things together. Jason would take Arnold across the street to the playground to play with the other children. Of course, he had to promise Mrs. Wilson not to drop him. And Arnold really liked these trips... in spite of the fact he got dizzy rolling down the sliding board and often bounced off the see-saw.

The Wilson's weren't ready for the next step. "Can Arnold join Boy Scouts?" Jason asked. The Wilson's weren't sure. "Does he meet the joining requirements?"

"He may be only a *head*," Jason responded, "but he's an *eleven year old* head."

So it came to be that Arnold attended his first Boy Scout Meeting and officially became a Boy Scout. It was a great experience and though there were many things that Arnold couldn't do, he and the Troop made the best of it. He was really proud the day when he was elected as Patrol Leader of the New Boy Patrol.

"You might say that now I'm officially the *head* of the patrol," he joked.

Now Scouting wasn't easy for Arnold. He loved the camping... but the hikes were kind of rough. He'd always need help on the uphill parts where the other Scouts were willing to oblige by kicking him along... and though he'd always slow them down... he'd make it up on the downhill parts when he'd roll right past them.

And Arnold still remembers his Scoutmaster's words when he received his Tenderfoot Badge. "They say that Scouting rounds a boy out — and nobody shows that better than our newest Tenderfoot Scout, Arnold."

But Scouting... and life in general... still had its disappointments for Arnold. There were so many things that he wanted to do that he couldn't, just because he was only a *head*. If only he could be a normal boy with arms and legs like Jason and the rest of the Scouts. Then he wouldn't feel like such a burden. He'd be able to swim without bobbing like a cork. But despite these occasional feelings, Arnold hung in there. He was a real fighter.

Then one day it got to be too much. Arnold was perched in his bay window looking out at the children playing and laughing in the playground across the street. They were having such a good time... and all he could do was just sit there in his bowl. He wanted so much to be like them... to have a body with arms and legs. He was tired of just being a *head.*

Arnold closed his eyes real tight and he wished real hard, "I wish I had a real body like all the other children." He kept his eyes shut real tight and all of a sudden he heard this big "POOF". Arnold opened his eyes and looked down. He had a body... He had arms... He had legs... And he even had clothes on. For the first time in his life he was a real boy. He was so excited. He couldn't wait to tell all of his friends in the playground across the street.

Arnold bolted for the door. Opened it. Then ran straight for the playground.

The children in the playground were startled by the screeching of brakes, followed by a loud thud. A car had struck a child who was running into the street. Yes, Arnold got hit by a car... and was killed.

"I never saw him," the driver exclaimed. "He never looked."

Arnold had never had to learn how to cross a street. Nobody had ever taught him the dangers.

Though this was a very sad moment, Arnold's family and friends looked on the bright side. Arnold had overcome so much adversity in his short life... beating all of the odds... to bring so much joy into the lives of others. He proved that children could become friends despite their differences.

There's also a message here for all of us. Life is not always fair. You need to accept yourself for what you are and make the best of it. Wishing that you are like others may not be the best solution. So, if you every find yourself in this situation, think about Arnold and remember "sometimes it's better to quit while you're a head."

AN ADDICTION TO TEA

For centuries before America was discovered, whether by Christopher Columbus in 1492 or Lief Erickson years earlier, the lands were inhabited by Indians. Now these Indians may not have lived in the custom or style of the Europeans, but they did have a culture of their own. They always made the most of their environment in tending to their needs. The eastern Indians who greeted the early settlers had already established self-supporting villages. They used the elements — wood and earth — for making dwellings. They hunted animals for food and clothing. They raised crops such as corn and tobacco, which were unknown in Europe at the time, using fertilizer techniques, such as dead fish, that they had developed. They used many herbs and plants for medicinal purposes. Yes, the Indians were doing well before the settlers came.

When the settlers came in the early 1600's, they exposed the Indians to many new things. Some of these were good and helped the Indians to improve their way of life. Others were not so good. They exposed the Indians to new diseases and products that caused the Indians health problems. As the new settlers and the Indians learned to live together they continued to trade products and ideas. As new products became available in Europe, they were soon transferred to the Colonies, and then the Indians. This trading became a way of life for generations.

Unlike their farming cousins in the east, it took probably another hundred years for the nomadic Indians in the west to be exposed to many of the settler's ways. Tribes such as the Sioux had established their own culture and way of life. They used animal skins for making portable houses, called tepees. They used horses, which had been introduced to America by the Spaniards, for transportation. For the most part, they were very suspicious and distrustful of new things. As the settlers moved west, they traded many things to the Indians for the fine hides and furs of the animals. Not all of these things were good. They introduced the Indians to rifles and gunpowder... alcohol... and one of their favorites — tea.

Now, tea had always been a favorite drink of the settlers as evidenced in history. After all, it was the extravagant tax on tea by England which led to the Boston Tea Party and eventually the Revolutionary War. But the colonists had been drinking tea for generations, and were well aware of the side effects caused by one of tea's main ingredients — caffeine. They were aware that the more you drank tea, the more you would have to go to the bathroom. Unfortunately, the Indians were not yet aware of these problems.

Chief Hunting Bear was a well respected Sioux Chief whose tribe frequently traded with the settlers who passed their village in wagon trains heading west. Their tepees contained many items that the settlers had exchanged for hides or trinkets. Many of the Indians liked the new woven materials that the settlers had. Chief Hunting Bear liked the tea. His tepee was stocked with several cases of tea which he and his tribe had acquired from the settlers.

This affliction started years earlier when the first settlers moved into the territory. Wanting to make friends with the local Indians, the settlers invited Chief Hunting Bear and a few of his braves to their homes for some food and beverage. Of course, the beverage of choice was tea. At first the Indians were reluctant to try, but when they saw the settlers drinking and enjoying this strange new beverage, they yielded.

"Ummh, this is good!" exclaimed Chief Hunting Bear. From that day on he was hooked.

The settlers saw that Chief Hunting Bear liked the tea so much that they gave him some to take back to his tepee. At first Chief Hunting Bear drank the tea only when the settlers visited his village for trading when he'd invite them into his tepee for a drink. But soon, he began to like this new beverage so much that he began to drink it at every meal... and then at all hours of the day. Drinking tea had become an obsession for Chief Hunting Bear. He had formed an addiction to the stuff. The members of his tribe hardly saw him any more — except for his frequent trips, sometimes at a full run, to the woods to relieve himself. None of the settlers had ever told him of the side effects.

The members of Chief Hunting Bear's tribe were growing very concerned. They appealed to the Chief to stop drinking the tea, but he wouldn't listen. He liked it too much. They appealed to the settlers to stop trading tea to the tribe — and the settlers tried — but Chief

Hunting Bear became very angry. He wanted his tea! The settlers relented. Chief Hunting Bear was a powerful chief and the settlers were afraid that he might start trouble if he didn't get his tea. So they continued to provide it.

Finally, they decided to appeal to Chief Hunting Bear for health reasons. The town doctor visited the village and requested a meeting with Chief Hunting Bear. At first Chief Hunting Bear declined, but, out of friendship to the settlers, finally invited the doctor into his tepee. He also invited the other tribe elders, including the medicine man. They sat in council... ate... and drank — you guessed it — tea.

The doctor tried to explain the bad side of drinking tea... the fact that it contained caffeine which was addictive... created dependencies... and made you have to frequently go to the bathroom. He tried to put this in terms that Chief Hunting Bear and the other Indians could understand. Chief Hunting Bear just nodded... stood up and started chanting and doing this uncontrollable jig.

"That's quite a dance," the doctor thought to himself, but in a moment Chief Hunting Bear stopped, excused himself, left the tepee, and went running for the woods.

When the chief returned, looking relieved, he thanked the doctor for his concern. He then had the other Indians escort the doctor from the tepee while he stayed behind to drink more tea. The talk had done no good. The Chief wouldn't listen.

The doctor felt somewhat guilty. After all, it was the settlers who had first introduced Chief Hunting Bear to tea. He asked the medicine man to please keep an eye on the chief and to come get him if there was ever a problem. The medicine man promised he would.

For the next several weeks the medicine man kept a close watch on his chief. Chief Hunting Bear rarely ventured from his tepee now, except for his runs to the tree line, that were now becoming more frequent... or to yell to his braves to bring him more tea. Several times the medicine man tried to talk to the chief, but if he ever brought up the subject of tea, the chief became very angry. The chief wouldn't listen.

Then it happened. One morning the medicine man noticed that Chief Hunting Bear had not been leaving his tepee to make his runs to the tree line. This was very unusual. Something must be wrong. He summoned some braves and went to Chief Hunting Bear's tepee to investigate. They called — but there was no answer. The medicine man opened the tepee flap and peeked through. He screamed.

Quickly, the medicine man sent braves into town to get the doctor who, true to his promise, responded immediately. He went with the medicine man to see Chief Hunting Bear. Together, they looked through the open flap, but it was too late. Chief Hunting Bear was dead.

He had drowned in his tea pee.

MULBERRY MANSION

Troop 473 was looking forward to camping at the Mulberry Mansion, if you wanted to call sleeping in an old Victorian house camping. The Mulberry Mansion was built in the late 1800's and had been in the Mulberry family for generations. It was located on the Mulberry Estate on top of a small hill on the outskirts of town. The present Mr. Mulberry was very fond of Scouting and often let Scout groups camp on the premises — and in the winter they could use the mansion. He, himself, lived in a modern mansion on the other side of the estate.

This was the ideal place for winter fun. The sleigh riding on the hill outside the mansion was the best around... and down at the bottom was a lake which normally was frozen at this time of year. Scout groups always brought their sleds and ice skates. And if you got cold you just went inside the mansion, for there were at least four stone fireplaces to keep you warm; that is, if you had enough firewood. Mr. Mulberry, however, always did his best to make sure there was an ample supply on hand for the Scouts.

On the downside, there was no electricity and little furniture. The house was lit by oil lamps... and there were no TV's, stereo's, or other such reminders of the present day. The Scouts cooked in a country kitchen on a wood stove and slept on the floors in one of the mansion's many rooms. Nobody seemed to know how many there were on the mansion's three floors, but there were many. This just added to the mystique — the adventure of it all.

All of the Scouts were excited on the weekend of the big campout. It was snowing and cold. You couldn't ask for any better weather for staying at the mansion. When the Scouts met at the Scout Hall at six o'clock, it was already dark, and the snow was several inches deep. They loaded their gear into the trucks and then sat back for the short drive to the Mulberry Estate. They were there in a half hour.

"Wow," said Johnny, as they drove through the big gate at the entrance. "This place is huge."

Ten minutes later the Scouts were driving past the frozen lake when one of the boys spotted the mansion.

"Look!" he shouted as he excitedly pointed. The large building with its pointed spires was easy to see at the top of the hill. The full moon cast eerie shadows in the glistening snow. "It looks haunted." The other boys laughed.

They parked the vehicles on the side of the house. Mr. Mulberry said he would leave the key in the mailbox, immediately inside the wrought iron picket fence... and it was there like he said. "Probably hasn't been any mail delivered to this place in a hundred years," thought the Scoutmaster.

The Scouts brought all the gear into the house and then scampered with their sleeping bags to find a good spot to sleep, as the adults lit as many of the oil lamps as they could find. The rooms with the fireplaces were all top choices. Fortunately, there were several of them — enough for each of the three patrols, plus one for the adults. Unfortunately, they were spread throughout the building. It was like an Easter egg hunt trying to find them. The Scouts thought it was "cool".

Afterward, they regrouped in the kitchen for a snack before going to bed. "You need to get a good night's sleep," the Scoutmaster told them. "We have a long day ahead of us tomorrow." With that they headed back to their respective rooms and crawled into their sleeping bags.

Johnny couldn't sleep. He laid in his sleeping bag watching the eerie red shadows that the flames from the fireplace cast around the room. "This place gives me the creeps." He closed his eyes. Johnny tried everything but he just couldn't doze off. Now it was the noises. He swore he could hear clocks ticking and boards creaking. He closed his eyes tighter. That's when he heard it.

A deep, scary voice echoed through the building saying "It floats on water!"

Johnny screamed.

The screams awakened the rest of the patrol. They rushed to see what was the matter. Johnny told them that he heard somebody yelling "It floats on water!"

The other boys laughed. Nobody else had heard anything. "Go back to sleep," they told him. "You were dreaming."

"No I wasn't," Johnny said defiantly, "I heard it... and it was scary."

By now everybody else had returned to their sleeping bags to try to get back to sleep. Johnny just laid there saying to himself over and over again "I know I heard it. I know I heard it. It floats on water!"

The next morning all the Scouts met in the kitchen and looked ready to tackle a day of winter fun. Everybody except Johnny, that is. He hardly got a wink of sleep all night and he looked it. He kept wondering who was yelling "It floats on water"... and, more importantly, what ***it*** was? However, he did his best to participate in the activities. There was a foot of new snow on the ground and so much to do outdoors.

"Good," Johnny thought. Outdoors was where he wanted to be. Anywhere away from the Mulberry Mansion.

The Scouts spent the morning sleigh riding and the afternoon ice skating. They even chose sides for a short game of hockey. Johnny didn't play. He used the time to take a short nap.

That evening the Scouts played some games and then the patrols retired to their respective rooms to sleep. As they crawled into their sleeping bags one of the boys yelled sarcastically at Johnny "It floats on water" and then made sounds like a ghost. The other Scouts laughed.

Johnny didn't think it was funny. Tonight Johnny tried to stay awake, but he was too tired and he fast dozed off. The afternoon nap wasn't long enough. Around midnight he was awakened by a noise. He listened.

"It floats on water!"

Johnny was going to scream, but he remembered what had happened the previous night. So he just laid there and listened. Again he wondered what ***it*** was?

"It floats on water!"

He heard it again. This time louder and closer. It was coming from right outside his door. Now he screamed.

The scream awoke the other boys who ran to Johnny's side. "I heard it again," he said. The Scouts laughed, annoyingly — then they heard it!

"It floats on water!"

They, along with Johnny, ran for the door, but just as they arrived, Alex jumped out in front of them.

"Boo!"

They all jumped.

"It floats on water!" he yelled. It had been him all the time.

After their initial scare, the boys laughed about it and went back to sleep. Not Johnny. He wasn't convinced.

Johnny wasn't disappointed. An hour later he heard it again... and this time in the same deep, scary voice of the night before.

"It floats on water!"

He sat up and looked around the room. This time several other Scouts were sitting up in their sleeping bags, including Alex.

"It floats on water!"

This time everyone heard it. The Scouts all grabbed their flashlights. They were going to make an attempt to track down the source of the sound. "Stay together!" the Patrol Leader cautioned.

"It floats on water!"

It seemed to be coming from the floor above. The Scouts moved in that direction. Suddenly, they froze. There was noise coming from the hallway directly ahead, and it was coming directly toward them.

Johnny's patrol prepared to run. Just then the rest of the Troop's Scouts came running around the corner from the hall ahead. They had heard the sound too and were going to investigate.

"It floats on water!" echoed through the house in that same deep, scary voice. It appeared to be coming from the attic.

Slowly the Scouts climbed the attic stairs, the light of some fourteen flashlights providing the only illumination. Their flashlights searching the attic looked like a London air raid during World War II.

They jumped as the door to the attic slammed below them. There was now no way out.

"It floats on water!" reverberated throughout the room.

Finally, Johnny screamed "I can't take it any more! What floats on water?"

After a moment of silence, the Scouts heard the response.

"Ivory soap!"

(Note to the teller: Make sure you say the words 'It floats on water' in a deep scary voice... and then use the same voice to say 'Ivory soap'.)

HUNTING BEARS

John Stevens had never been a Scoutmaster before. He'd never even been a Boy Scout. But he loved kids... loved the outdoors... and had lots of experience as a Sunday School teacher. So how could he say no when his church asked him to take charge of the Troop. Besides the Troop was down to ten active boys and the church was afraid they might have to close the Troop if they didn't find a Scoutmaster soon. Mr. Stevens decided he'd give it his best shot.

The first few months were spent getting some additional adult help, getting to know the boys, and getting some training. He attended Scoutmaster Fundamentals and learned everything he could about running a Boy Scout Troop or I should say having the boys run the Troop.

The boy leaders had been doing a good job of planning and running the Troop Meetings and attendance had actually increased. Now it was time for their first campout.

"Well, boys," he said at their next planning session, "I think it's time we planned a campout."

"Great!" the boy leaders responded in unison. "It's been too long since our last one." The Troop had been in the habit of monthly camping when they were going strong, but they hadn't been camping much with their adult leadership problems.

"So Mr. Stevens, where are we going?"

"That's for you to tell me. You guys are the leaders." Mr. Stevens was proud of himself. He was letting the boys run things, just like he had learned in his training.

"Wow, we'll have to think that over," replied Joey, the Senior Patrol Leader. He quickly motioned for the other boy leaders to huddle up. Mr. Stevens watched as they mumbled lowly amongst themselves. They were talking and giggling, but after ten minutes they came back to the table.

"We've decided," Joey said. "We'd like to go to Mountain Lake State Park. It was unanimous."

"Okay, and why did you pick Mountain Lake?" Mr. Stevens queried.

"Because that's where the bears are!"

Now Mr. Stevens didn't camp much, but he still knew the outdoors, and to the best of his knowledge there were no bears in this area of the state. There were plenty of woods... but the mountains were really hills, not really the habitat for bears. However, not wanting to dull their enthusiasm, he asked, "Are you sure? I've never heard of bears in this area before."

"Uh huh," came the reply. "We've been there before and we've seen them."

How could Mr. Steven argue with this? A campout at Mountain Lake State Park was put on the calendar for next month. The boys couldn't wait. Neither could Mr. Stevens. The Troop Leader's Council planned the campout program. Mr. Stevens noticed that it was a good mix of Scouting skills and free time... complete with time set aside on Saturday afternoon for a *bear hunt*.

"That ought to prove interesting," Mr. Stevens thought.

Well, the weekend of the campout came. The Scouts met on Friday evening, loaded the gear, then got into the cars for the two hour ride to Mountain Lake State Park. There were eight boys and two adults. It was after eight when the Troop arrived at the park and were escorted to the campsite by the ranger. While the Scouts set up camp, Mr. Stevens called the Ranger aside.

"Are there any bears up here?"

The ranger laughed. He confirmed that to the best of his knowledge, and he'd been at the park for eight years, there had never been a bear in the park. Mr. Stevens felt reassured.

The next morning the Scouts had breakfast and then began to follow the program that they had planned. They spent the morning working with some of the younger boys on their badges and then stopped for lunch.

"It's a beautiful day, isn't it?" Joey observed.

Joey was right. The sun was shining bright and the temperature was pushing 90 degrees.

"That's good because the hot weather really brings out the bears," Joey continued. The older boys laughed.

After lunch he rounded up the boys and told them to go get their bear hunting equipment, if they had any. A few of the older boys went to their tents and returned with day packs. Joey explained the rules.

"The idea is to see which Scout can see the most bears. Remember, the object is to see the bears without them seeing you. We'll travel in pairs."

On Joey's signal the Scouts paired up and began heading for the trail which led to the lake. Mr. Stevens and his Assistant got up and began to follow.

"Whoa," Joey said, "Bear hunting is a boy thing. No adults allowed. We'll be back in two hours."

Mr. Stevens was disappointed. He really wanted to see what they were going to do, since he knew there weren't any bears. But he also remembered, the boys were in charge, and he didn't see any harm in them having fun.

"Okay. But stay together and everybody be back in two hours."

As they headed down the trail, Joey made sure that each boy had a partner... and he made sure that each of the newer scouts was with an older boy who had been *bear hunting* before. Joey himself took Peter, the youngest scout in the Troop. "I'll show you the techniques," he told him.

In a half mile the trail forked. A marker indicated that the State Park swimming area was to the left. Joey indicated that the bears were to the right. About ten minutes later, Joey motioned for the boys to get down. They were getting close. He could see the signs. The only signs that Peter could see said "No Trespassing" and "Keep Out".

"Here's where we split up," Joey said. "Remember, you have about 45 minutes to see as many bears as you can. Then we meet back here." They were off.

Joey was heading for the lake, cutting straight through the woods. Then he and Peter heard it. There were sounds coming from the woods in front of them. Joey motioned for Peter to get down.

"Stay here. I'll go check it out," Joey said to Peter. Then he headed toward the noise.

Peter stayed right where he was told. He was a little scared.

Then he heard the screams. Loud piercing screams. Followed by the sound of someone running through the woods. Peter looked up. It was Joey. His shirt was torn and his face was covered with scratches. He was yelling "Run, Peter! Run!"

Peter didn't have to be told twice. He ran as fast as he could back to the signs where he was to meet the other boys. They were already there. They, too, had heard the screams and came to see what was the matter. They waited for Joey... but Joey never came. After twenty minutes they thought it best to go back to camp and tell Mr. Stevens. They ran as fast as they could, every now and then looking back to see if they were being followed.

"Mr. Stevens, Mr. Stevens! The bears got Joey." The boys were all excited.

"I saw it, Mr. Stevens!" Peter exclaimed. "Joey was cut and bleeding."

Mr. Stevens left with the older boys to investigate. They reached the signs in fifteen minutes, but there was still no sign of Joey. Mr. Stevens wondered what they were doing anyway ignoring these "No Trespassing" and "Keep Out" signs. They spread out and began looking around.

"Look! Over there!" shouted one of the boys.

Sure enough. There was a small pack tangled in the briars. The boys were able to identify it as Joey's bear hunting pack. Funny, all it contained was a pair of binoculars. But wait, nearby were pieces of torn clothing.

"That's what Joey was wearing," cried Peter.

"This looks serious," Mr. Stevens remarked. "We'd better go back and tell the ranger." They all headed back toward camp.

As they neared the campsite they could see the ranger's vehicle pulling into the parking area.

"Good! It will save us the phone call."

The ranger left his car and started walking toward Mr. Stevens. The ranger spoke first.

"Understand you might be missing a boy?"

"Yes, we think the bears got him," replied Mr. Stevens with a sense of dread.

The ranger laughed.

"You're close. The BARES got him. He was caught snooping on the private nudist beach on the other side of the lake."

Mr. Stevens looked and Joey was now emerging from the back seat of the ranger's vehicle and was talking to the other boys.

"He's a little scraped up. He ran through some briar patches trying to get away and twisted his ankle. The nudists helped him and then called me to pick him up. I think he was more embarrassed than they were."

"Thanks. I'll have a good long talk with him and the rest of the boys — no more bare hunts!"

RETURN OF THE MIST

It was early June and Troop 742 was participating in the Council's Gold Rush Camporee. The Scouts had a wonderful time participating in the many "Old West" events being conducted by the program staff. There were panning for gold, lasso throwing, burro racing, rifle shooting and lots more. It was a shame the day's activities were coming to an end, but at least that would bring the campfire. The staff had planned a spectacular campfire for the closing. They dressed like cowboys, led the Scouts in western songs, and performed skits with a western theme. The highlight of the campfire, however, was the campfire story.

An elderly Scouter with a scraggly white beard, and dressed like a prospector, told the Scouts the story about the Valley of the Blue Mist. It was the story of three boys who, over a hundred years ago, decided to head west to find their fortune in gold. They had tried several places but they were always too crowded — until they stumbled onto this river near an abandoned tent camp. At first they thought the camp must have been abandoned because there was no gold... so they were surprised when their panning yielded their biggest find yet. That's when a nearby prospector told them "You need not be surprised boys. You may not be here long either. There are things more important than gold! But whatever you do as long as you stay in this valley, get into your tents by nightfall. Don't get caught by the blue mist. People die who get caught by it." The storyteller went on to tell how the blue mist made everyone get violently sick until they died a horrible death. At first the three boys heeded the old man's warning, but eventually they left the tent camp for an old cabin further up the hill. The old man warned them that the cabin was okay during the day, but at night... the blue mist would come and kill. One by one the boys disregarded the warning... and one by one they died. Eventually the prospectors found that the cabin was built over a mine entrance to conceal a large gold vein, the 'mother lode', but the mine contained a pocket of deadly gas. Every night as the blue mist settled on the valley, the gas escaped from the mine and killed everyone who breathed it. The storyteller had the boys' attention the whole time. It was great.

After the campfire everyone returned to their tent area to get ready for bed... and just in time because a heavy mist was beginning to settle to the ground.

"Hurry, get to bed!" I jokingly yelled. "Don't get caught out of your tent in the blue mist... or else you'll die."

The Scouts all laughed as they zipped up their tents and crawled into their sleeping bags.

"They ought to sleep well," I thought as I crawled into my own sleeping bag, "it has been a long day."

I was wrong. At about twelve-thirty in the morning I was awakened by a faint cry outside my tent.

"Mr. Crabtree! Mr. Crabtree!"

I looked outside to find Billy, our newest Scout. Obviously every one didn't sleep well. "What's up, Billy?" I asked.

"I think it's the mist... the blue mist. We must have pitched our patrol site near a mine entrance."

"Huh," I said, being caught a little off guard.

Billy continued, "I woke up and I couldn't breath. There was this awful smell."

I grabbed my flashlight, got out of my tent, and asked Billy to take me to his patrol area. There was still a heavy mist around the campsite... but it didn't look blue. We were there in a minute.

"Everything looks fine to me, Billy. I think maybe you were dreaming."

"I don't think so. I smelled it."

"Why don't you just get back to your tent and try to go back to sleep?"

A Scout is obedient... so Billy obeyed, though I believe he would rather have not. I returned to my tent and my warm sleeping bag. "I sure hope this fog lifts by morning," I thought.

An hour later I was awakened again.

"Mr. Crabtree." *Cough* "Mr. Crabtree." I recognized the voice. It was the same one I had heard earlier. I shined my light out of the tent. Billy was standing there with his hands to his nose and mouth, gagging.

"It's the blue mist, Mr. Crabtree. It's in my tent. It's in our whole campsite."

"No more stories for you, Billy," I thought to myself as I slowly exited my tent to take Billy back. The mist was still in the air. "Let's go check it out," I said as

I wondered what story I would use this time to get Billy back to sleep.

This time, however, as I neared Billy's tent, I, too, began to catch wind of this awful stench. I quickly put my hands to my nose. I was not alone. I could hear stirring in a few of the other tents and within seconds Billy and I were joined by two other Scouts who were gagging.

That's when we heard it. The sound of escaping gas. It was coming from several areas of the campsite at once.

"It's the blue mist. It's going to kill us all!" said Billy holding his nose.

I wasn't so sure, but I had a hunch.

"We need to find the source of this activity." I motioned for the boys to follow me to the dining area.

They sat at the picnic table, doing their best to breath deep in the clean fresh air, while I looked around for clues. There it was just as I suspected. I removed the cans from the trash and placed them on the table. The three boys gathered round.

"Your patrol had beans for supper tonight, didn't they?"

They all nodded yes.

"Go get your sleeping bags and sleep over here. Everything will be okay."

THE GLOOP MAKER

(This is my version of a story I'm told is a favorite around British campfires.)

Back in the early 1800's, ships were made out of wood and had huge sails to make them go. They didn't have the motors and guidance equipment that we have today. Back then the ships were built tough — and the men that sailed them were even tougher. Everybody's life depended on the operation of the ship and the work of each and every seaman.

For as long as he could remember Marvin Glasser had wanted to be a sailor. He often laid awake dreaming about sailing the seven seas... traveling to far away places... and gaining the admiration of all the girls who just adored sailors. Many days he would stroll down to the docks to look at the masted boats in all their glory, fantasizing what it would be like to sail them out to sea. There was only one problem, however, Marvin hated work. He really dreaded the thought of any type of manual labor and thus his fantasy remained a dream.

Then one day on one of his strolls down to the docks to admire the ships, Marvin observed a sailor precariously hanging over the side of the ship caulking the seams in the hull.

"You'd never get me to do that," Marvin thought, "that looks too dangerous."

Before Marvin could have another thought, the sailor slipped and fell into the water alongside the dock.

"Help! Help!" Marvin screamed, but there was nobody else around.

Quickly, Marvin grabbed a long plank which was lying nearby and extended it over the dock to the sailor in the waters below. With a mighty yank he pulled the sailor to safety, mere moments before a wave pushed the ship firmly against the dock.

"I would have been crushed," said the sailor. "Killed without a doubt. Thank you, sir. Is there anything I can do to repay you?"

"This is my chance," thought Marvin. "Perhaps now I can become a sailor." He turned to the sailor and said, "I'd like to sail out to sea. Can you get me a job on your ship?"

"Well, I don't know," the sailor said, checking out Marvin's rather frail physique. "The crew is pretty full at this time."

"But I saved your life... and I'm willing to work." Marvin could hardly believe he said that last statement, but he was getting desperate.

"And just what is it you do, lad?"

Marvin thought for a moment and then blurted, "I'm a gloop maker."

This startled the sailor for a second. "What's a gloop maker?" he thought to himself, trying not to show his ignorance in front of Marvin.

"Hmmm, I'm not sure we have one of those. Let's go speak to the Bosun's Mate."

So Marvin and the sailor walked up the gang plank onto the old ship and tracked down the Bosun's Mate. He was a mountain of a man with a dark black beard and a face weathered by ocean storms.

"What do you want?" he scowled. "I've got work to do."

"Oh, that word again," Marvin thought.

"Bosun, this lad would like to sail with us."

"Ha, ha, ha!" the Bosun laughed. "What can this scrawny boy do to help us?"

"He's the world's greatest gloop maker," the sailor replied, "and we don't have any of those."

The Bosun stopped laughing and put his hand to his chin. "What the heck is a gloop maker," he thought, but he didn't want to say anything for fear of looking stupid in front of his sailors.

"You're right. We don't have any gloop makers. But only the Captain can hire the crew. We'll have to go see the captain."

So Marvin and the Bosun's Mate left for the Captain's cabin. It was way on the other side of the boat. Along the way Marvin looked at all of the other sailors working hard to get the ship ready to sail. "Ughh," he thought.

Knock, knock.

"Come in," said the Captain.

Marvin and the Bosun entered.

"And what is this, Bosun? Why are you bringing me this boy?"

"He's looking for a job on the ship, Captain."

"We need men, not boys."

"But he's the world's greatest gloop maker and

we don't have any of those. Every ship needs a gloop maker."

"The Bosun's right," the Captain thought, "we don't have one of those. As a matter of fact, I don't know what one of those is. Just what is a gloop maker?"

However, not wanting to let his Bosun know this, he exclaimed, "By all means, hire the lad, and give him everything he needs. We sail tomorrow... and we sail with the world's greatest gloop maker on board."

Early the next morning, the ship set sail. At long last Marvin was experiencing his dream... but it didn't take long before his dream became a nightmare.

"You mean this is where we sleep?" Marvin asked, pointing to the crowded crews quarters where hammocks were strung in every available spot. "I can't sleep here. Gloop makers need room to work. I need my own cabin."

The other sailors laughed, but Marvin's complaints reached the Captain. "Give the gloop maker his own cabin," he ordered. "We don't want anything to keep us from having the world's greatest gloop." And so Marvin got his own private cabin with a bed and a door. The Captain even had "Gloop Maker" painted on the door so that the other sailors would not disturb him while he worked.

Marvin was often seen by the other sailors walking the ship's decks. Many accused him of doing nothing... a stowaway they called him. Marvin said he was looking for new materials for making the gloop. Often he asked for tools and other supplies... copper, tin, and wood... to be brought to his cabin. And sometimes you could hear banging echoing through the ship.

"Maybe he *is* making a gloop," they thought.

Still it seemed that every time the weather turned nasty... or there was a watch to do... or work to be done... Marvin would retreat to his cabin.

"Time to get back to working on my gloop," he would say.

Even the Bosun and the Captain were beginning to grow impatient. For weeks they had been giving the gloop maker everything and still no gloop.

"World Class gloop's take time. Be patient!" Marvin exclaimed.

Finally, the Captain called the Bosun and Marvin into his quarters to discuss progress on the gloop.

"The men are about to mutiny," he said. "I need to know when the gloop will be ready. I need to know and I need to know now."

Marvin could see that the Captain was serious.

"The gloop will be ready this coming Saturday, sir."

From that day on the sailors could see a frenzy of activity as Marvin took more and more materials to his cabin. The banging noise echoed through the ship at all hours of the day and night. The sailors couldn't wait to see the gloop. Finally Saturday came.

The Captain assembled the entire crew on deck for this long awaited occasion. At last they were going to see the world's greatest gloop. He gave a short speech, followed by a blare from the ship trumpet. At this point the gloop maker emerged from his cabin to thundering applause carrying this large object covered by a blanket. Slowly he walked to the bow, shunning any attempts to help.

"What does a gloop look like?" everyone thought.

Marvin reached the gangplank. At that point, he removed the blanket. Everyone stared in amazement. It looked like a pile of junk, nailed and hammered together.

"Is that a gloop?"

"Boo! Hiss!"

The sailors were getting unruly, but Marvin, the gloop maker, raised his hand to silence them. He wasn't done yet. Slowly he carried this pile of junk to the end of the gang plank... fully extended his arms... and let go.

Everyone stared.

The great big mass fell straight down into the water making a sound which could be heard over the entire ship.

GLOOP!

TALE OF A GOOD MAN

Samuel Mason was a good man.

And why not? He was raised in a good family which cared for him and taught him good values. He was a straight "A" student in school, participated in many clubs, and attended church and Sunday school regularly. Of course, Samuel Mason had been a Cub Scout where he had many of his family values reinforced. His mother was a Den Leader and his father helped out wherever needed... the perfect example for a boy like Samuel.

Samuel Mason was a good man.

It was Boy Scouts, however, where Samuel learned leadership and developed his sense of adventure. He loved the outdoors. He had exceptional people skills and could communicate well with young boys and adult Scoutleaders equally as well. It was no wonder that in four short years Samuel had achieved the rank of Eagle Scout. He continued to serve his Troop until high school graduation.

Samuel Mason was a good man.

Samuel left Scouting when he went away to college to major in Political Science. He wanted to further develop his people skills and to prepare himself for a job in Government where he could continue his service to his country. He joined the Alpha Phi Omega service fraternity, continuing his service to the community. Though his grades were exceptional, he felt there was something missing. He missed the adventure that he had so enjoyed as a Boy Scout. He missed the thrill of seeing new places... and doing new things. So it was no surprise that after graduating near the top of his class, Samuel decided to postpone his career and enlist in the Peace Corps.

Samuel Mason was a good man.

The Peace Corps was no picnic. Samuel had to undergo months of rigorous training... language training, cultural training, and physical training. But as usual, Samuel excelled. Finally, he was ready. He was assigned to a Peace Corp expedition to the deepest parts of the Amazon Rain Forest in South America. There he would have the opportunity to use his skills to help some of the poorest people in the world.

Samuel Mason was a good man.

Samuel lived in a grass hut in a small village deep within the rain forest. He worked with the villagers to build new houses. He taught them about sanitation and farming techniques. He really impressed his supervisors with his ability to communicate with the people in the community and they were amazed at how well they accepted him. Perhaps it was the way Samuel worked with the village children... or the way he worked with the villagers, always helping with projects, not just supervising. Skills he had learned in Scouting were paying off.

Samuel Mason was a good man.

Probably, Samuel's most important accomplishment while he was in South America was negotiating a truce between neighboring tribes who had been fighting for generations. Both tribes respected Samuel for his caring. He could be trusted. He was able to bring the warring chieftains together and work out a plan for peace... a peace that was still intact when his two year assignment was done and he returned to the United States.

Samuel Mason was a good man.

Well, Samuel Mason had wanted a taste of adventure and he got it, but now it was time for him to settle down. He moved to Washington, D. C. and took a job with the State Department. At long last, he could start his Government career. He could continue to serve his country and make the world a better place to live.

Samuel Mason was a good man.

Settling down and working a steady job also gave Samuel Mason the time to again get involved with the one activity that he missed most over the past several years — Scouting. He volunteered his services with a local Boy Scout Troop; first serving as an Assistant Scoutmaster and then as Scoutmaster. It really felt great getting back to working with the boys. He still loved the camping... and the adventure of it all. He was really making his mark on the community.

Samuel Mason was a good man.

But duty called again and he had to leave. Rival terrorist groups were creating havoc in the Middle East and there was only one man that the State Department could rely upon to negotiate a truce — Samuel Mason. He would have to leave immediately. The State Department wanted him to convince the leaders to stop their terrorist activities. Samuel really didn't want to go, but he felt he had to. He had to go and serve his country.

Samuel Mason was a good man.

It was a sixteen hour plane ride to the Middle East and though the task at hand seemed ominous Samuel still couldn't pass up the opportunity to help others. He courteously helped people place their luggage in the overhead compartments and surrendered his aisle seat to an old lady in exchange for her cramped window seat. This was so Scout-like. You would never guess that the fate of world peace laid on his shoulders.

Samuel Mason was a good man.

The meeting with the terrorists went better than expected. The State Department was right. Samuel Mason was the man for the job. He met with the leaders continuously for several days. He earned their trust and respect. He urged them to compromise. He got them talking. Within a week the terrorists were at the bargaining table and a crisis was averted.

Samuel Mason was a good man.

He did such a good job that the State Department didn't want him to come home. There was trouble brewing in Africa and everyone knew that Samuel was the man who could save the day. They asked him and he agreed... but only after convincing them that he needed a few days off. Of course Samuel spent those precious days helping a local orphanage. He really missed working with his Scouts back in the states.

Samuel Mason was a good man.

The State Department had arranged for a small plane to take Samuel and five other people to their destination deep in the jungles of Africa. Flying time would be about four hours on this two engine turboprop, except that after an hour the plane began experiencing difficulties. The right engine sputtered and eventually stopped. The plane began losing altitude. Samuel Mason used his Scout training and remained calm. He reassured the other passengers that everything would be okay. He opened the small rear door and began throwing luggage and other gear out. The plane stabilized.

Samuel Mason was a good man.

However, just as they began to celebrate they heard a loud sputtering noise coming from the left engine. Then it too stopped. The plane was now gliding unpowered to the earth. The pilot ordered the men to bail out. The plane was doomed to crash. All of the men started putting on their parachutes. That's when they discovered that they were one parachute short.

"It must have been thrown out by mistake with the other gear."

Samuel Mason took off his parachute and gave it to his friend. He didn't want to take it, but Samuel insisted. His friend strapped it to his back, said "goodbye", and jumped with his fellow passengers. Samuel sat down, strapped himself in, and prayed as the pilot tried to crash land the plane in the jungle.

Samuel Mason was a good man.

The plane was shaking violently and losing altitude fast. Samuel didn't look out the window because he didn't want to see what fate bestowed him. Then all of a sudden he heard the plane hit. Everything was dark and he could hear the sound of tree limbs breaking and plane parts falling off. After what seemed like an eternity the plane screeched to a halt. He was okay. He quickly unbuckled his seat belt and ran forward to check on the pilot. Unfortunately, the pilot was badly hurt. He had absorbed most of the impact. Samuel located a first aid kit and treated him, even though it looked hopeless. He stayed there and comforted him... until he died.

Samuel Mason was a good man.

Now he was alone in the jungle... but he had his wits and his Scout training. He gathered up what supplies he could from the plane and planned his strategy for survival. That night he camped near the plane, building a fire for heat. He didn't sleep much as he listened to the jungle sounds around him. Next morning he put his plan to action. First he climbed a tree and looked around. He didn't see any sign of life, but there was a river a short distance to the east. He headed in that direction reaching it in half an hour. Near the river he found a path, and on it were the tracks of people heading upstream. Samuel was elated and followed them.

Less than an hour later he could hear the sounds of drums. He quickened his pace. Then he saw it... straight ahead... a village. He began to run.

"I'm saved," he shouted.

As he neared the village he could make out the grass huts. They almost reminded him of the ones he had seen in the amazon. Then he saw the natives. They were sparsely dressed and carrying spears and shields. His shouts startled them and they ran to meet him. They gathered around and slowly escorted Samuel to the village. "Once again my Scouting skills have saved the day," he thought, as he helped one of the native boys who had fallen on the path.

Samuel Mason was a good man.

Samuel's sense of relief turned to terror as they reached the village. The ground was covered with what appeared to be human bones.

"These people are cannibals," he thought. He knew he was in trouble.

The villagers lead him to a grass hut and placed him under guard until they could bring their chief which they did shortly. Samuel tried to explain his predicament... the plane crash... and all that — but he wasn't getting through. The chief kept feeling Samuel's muscles. Finally, the chief invited Samuel for dinner — but deep down Samuel knew that he WAS the dinner.

He tried to use his negotiating skills. He explained that he was a good person and that it would not do them any good to eat him, but they just laughed.

"You'll all get sick," he yelled, but to no avail.

Samuel knew that his time was up, but if he was going to die, he was going to die with dignity. He even helped the villagers collect fire wood and to light the fire for their evening meal. Just maybe he was wrong.

Samuel Mason was a good man.

He also wasn't wrong. Samuel was the dinner meal... and the natives gobbled him down like they hadn't had a meal in weeks. Then one by one it happened. They began experiencing sharp pains in their stomachs until finally up it came. They all became violently sick, just like Samuel had warned.

Just goes to show "you really can't keep a good man down."

THE KIDNAPPING AT CAMP WHISPERING PINES

Boy Scout summer camp should be the highlight of every Troop's program year. A week in the woods doing Scouting things — swimming, fishing, canoeing, and working on lots of badges. Boy Scout camps pride themselves on this. They do the very best to provide Troops with the best possible camping facilities, program, and camping staff. Camp Whispering Pines was no different. They considered themselves to be the best. Therefore, it was extremely disappointing what Scout Jimmy Brady had to say.

It was the third day in camp and Jimmy Brady was on his way back from the beach when he had to go to the bathroom. He went into one of the stalls and closed the door. That's when he heard two adults talking about the "kidnapping". They were washing at the sinks and obviously unaware of his presence.

"I can't believe that we've had a "kidnapping" here at this summer camp," one of the adults said.

"Yeah! A real surprise," answered the other.

That's all that Jimmy could make out. He waited for the men to leave, then ran back to his campsite.

"Mr. Anderson! Mr. Anderson!" Jimmy was yelling when he entered the camp area. Mr. Anderson was his Scoutmaster.

He and the other adults and boys came running. They could tell from the sound of Jimmy's voice that something was wrong.

"Whoa, Jimmy," cried Mr. Anderson as he ran toward him. "What's the matter?"

Jimmy stopped for a moment to catch his breath, then blurted "There's been a kidnapping in camp. I heard some adults talking about it in the latrine."

Mr. Anderson was astonished... and angry. Astonished that a kidnapping could occur at a Boy Scout camp... and angry that neither he nor any of his other leaders had heard about it from the camp staff.

"If this is true, then we should have been warned to provide better protection for our Scouts."

Mr. Anderson decided to confront the camp staff. He left Jimmy at the campsite with his assistants and headed for the administration building. There, he confronted Mr. Bullock, the Camp Director for Camp Whispering Pines, a position he had held for the past five years.

Mr. Anderson laid it on the line. "Why weren't Scoutleaders told about the kidnapping in camp?"

Mr. Bullock looked astonished. "A kidnapping? At Camp Whispering Pines? Never!"

Mr. Bullock swore that neither he nor any of the camp staff had heard anything about a kidnapping. He assured Mr. Anderson that the camp had procedures in place to protect against such occurrences. But just to make sure, he would raise it as an issue at that evening's leaders' meeting.

Mr. Anderson felt better after leaving the administration building, but he still didn't know what to think. Jimmy was one of his most trustworthy Scouts and would not make up such a story... yet the camp staff would have no reason to lie about such an incident. Oh, well, he'd learn more later that night.

At supper both Jimmy and Mr. Anderson looked around the dining hall but everything looked normal; that is to say, chaotic. None of the troops seemed to be distressed. Jimmy had no idea which adults were involved. He had only heard voices — but he was sure of what they said.

Mr. Anderson left early for the leaders' meeting. He wanted to stop at the mail room first and see if the Troop had any mail. It was located just past the administration building to the rear. As he retrieved the Troop's mail he heard loud voices coming from the Camp Director's office. They were arguing. Mr. Anderson got close to the window so he could hear.

"They know about the kidnapping!" a voice clearly identifiable as the Camp Director bellowed.

"How?" answered another unidentifiable voice.

"Doesn't matter, they know. I don't know that I can keep it a secret anymore."

"But you promised... and we promised his parents. Besides you know the bad publicity that will come to the camp if they knew there was a kidnapping here."

"I know, but..."

"No 'buts'... you promised we'd keep it a secret."

With that the door closed and there was silence in the Camp Director's office.

"Gosh," thought Mr. Anderson from his hiding place outside the window, "there has been a kidnapping in camp... and the Camp Director is in on it." He didn't know what to do. He couldn't let on that he knew. Best to just attend the leaders' meeting for now. He went around to the front and entered the administration building. Most of the other leaders were already there.

Mr. Bullock discussed many things about the camp's activities but before he finished he said "There's been a report of a kidnapping in camp. I want to know if any of you know anything about it." Everybody in the room shook their head "no." Mr. Bullock thanked them and then dismissed the meeting.

All the way back to his campsite Mr. Anderson kept thinking about what he should do. Jimmy had heard there was a kidnapping... *he* had heard there was a kidnapping... and he could no longer trust the staff. He had to call in the authorities. Mr. Anderson stopped by the trading post to use the phone. His first phone call went to the local police, but they referred him to the Federal Bureau of Investigation, the FBI — kidnapping was a federal offense. He called them and told them the story.

The next day, just after lunch, a plain car pulled up in front of the administration building... and out emerged two men dressed in suits and wearing sun glasses. "Looks like FBI," one of the Scouts joked as he walked by. How right he was.

Agents Johnson and Frederico entered the building and asked to speak to the Camp Director. Two minutes after entering his office, an aide was sent to fetch Mr. Anderson. Ten minutes later, they were all gathered in the Camp Director's office. The agents wanted to hear the whole story and they wanted to hear the truth. Mr. Anderson started. He told about Jimmy... and then finished by telling about the Camp Director's conversation that he had overheard.

Mr. Bullock was visibly shaken. "Okay, okay! I admit it there has been a kidnapping in camp... but I was sworn to secrecy by the boy's parents... and by the Scoutmaster. Do you know the harm that would be done to this camp if Scouts and Scouters knew there was a kidnapping. I didn't know it was a federal offense. Follow me and I'll take you to the Troop involved." The agents and Mr. Anderson followed Mr. Bullock out of the door.

Mr. Bullock led them down the trail to Troop 837's campsite where they were met by Scoutmaster Troy Donahue. "What's up?" Troy asked.

"They know about the kidnapping," responded the Camp Director.

Mr. Donahue turned and led the men to a wall tent to the rear of camp. He flung open the flap and there in front of the men on a camp cot was — a kid napping.

"It's Scout Bobby Hendricks," Troy said, "and he was hoping that nobody would find out that he still takes a nap every day after lunch. His parents were afraid that the other Scouts would tease him."

"And we were afraid if Scouts and Scouters found out a kid was napping every day, that they'd question how challenging our program was," added the Camp Director.

"And we're afraid we came out here for nothing," said the agents.

The kidnapping case was closed.

THE SPIES

The generals who fought in the Revolutionary War to gain our freedom from England did not have the luxury of all the tools and gadgets of the generals of today. There were no spy satellites sending detailed pictures back to earth. There were no supersonic spy planes with their cameras and listening devices. The generals in the Revolutionary War had to gain their intelligence the old fashioned way — they used spies. This was not an easy task. The risks were high. Being caught as a spy behind enemy lines usually meant death.

The spy's job was also complicated by the variety of languages and dialects being used at the time. Everyone except the Indians who had a language of their own originated from somewhere else and either spoke their native language or spoke English with a heavy accent. This made it hard for the spy to gain information and also hard for him to communicate the facts back to his commanders who were often foreigners themselves.

Both the Colonists and the British employed the services of foreign Troops, either allied to them, or mercenaries who fought for a price... and both of them employed the services of spies to help them get information about enemy activities and intentions. This is the story of one general's attempt to get information and the problem of communications.

General Papillion had been in America for the past six months, having come to this country from France with a contingent of soldiers to help the Colonists' cause. He was a strong believer in freedom and, besides, he had no real love of the British. The Americans were ready to accept help from anyone and anywhere and welcomed General Papillion into their ranks with open arms. They bolstered his small contingent of Frenchmen with American volunteers. This joint group had distinguished themselves well during a few minor skirmishes along the Raritan River in New Jersey, but for the past two weeks they had been camped near New Brunswick, waiting. General Papillion sensed that something was up... it was TOO quiet. He assembled his officers.

"The British must be up to something. We've had no contact now for several weeks. We've got to find out what they're doing."

"Let's send in a spy," suggested one of his officers.

"A good idea, but it will have to be an American who is familiar with the area."

So it was that the decision was made. The Americans were polled and a brave volunteer selected. He was instructed to sneak behind the enemy lines, find out what the British were doing, and to report back to the general. He knew the risks, but these were dire times and that called for dire deeds. He left at dusk.

Late in the afternoon of the next day, the French sentries spotted a horse galloping up the rode. The rider was hanging in the saddle, barely able to stay upright as the horse sped along. As the rider approached they saw that it was the American spy so they let him past. Within moments the horse pulled up to the general's tent where the American collapsed to the ground. He had been severely wounded. General Papillion emerged from his tent and rushed with his aides to the wounded man's side.

As the aides tended to the American's wounds, the general asked, " The British... are they over there?"

The spy could hardly speak, so he just nodded his head.

"And are they massing for an attack?"

Again the spy nodded affirmatively.

Before the general could ask another question the spy reached out and pulled the general's head close to his mouth. Then with every ounce of strength he had left he uttered in his best attempt at a French accent, "watch out for the bacon tree!" Then he closed his eyes in death.

"Watch out for the bacon tree!" What could that possibly mean. General Papillion was bewildered. He had no choice but to send out another spy. Again he called for volunteers and another brave American stepped forward. He left immediately.

The next morning the sentries observed a lone man staggering up the road toward the perimeter of camp. They gave the challenge... and the man gave the proper reply... before falling to the ground. It was the American spy. He too had been severely wounded. He informed the sentries and they summoned the general.

Once again the French General came running with his aides. As the aides tended to the American's wounds, the general asked, " The British... are they over there?"

The American spy could hardly speak, so he just nodded his head.

"And are they massing for an attack?"

Again the spy nodded affirmatively. Then he opened his eyes wide and with a look of horror screamed in his best attempt at a French accent, "Watch out for the bacon tree!"

"What about the bacon tree?" the general asked in desperation, but it was too late. The spy had died.

Well, at least his two American spies had confirmed a few things — the British weren't far away and they were amassing for an attack. But he still did not know about this bacon tree. He had never heard of such a thing.

Once again General Papillion assembled his officers. He explained that the spies had confirmed that the British were near and that both had warned him to "watch out for the bacon tree." All of his officers were as bewildered as he was. Nobody had ever heard of a bacon tree. Finally, the general decided that the next day he would lead a small expeditionary force toward the enemy lines. He had to find out more about this bacon tree before launching a full scale attack.

So early the next morning, the general assembled twelve of his best troops. They were fully armed as they mounted their horses for this exploratory mission. They waved to the sentries as they made their way down the road toward where the spies had spotted the British. They traveled very slowly, trying to observe every little thing along the way. They really didn't know what they were looking for. Nobody had ever seen a bacon tree before.

They were about five miles down the road when all of a sudden everything got quiet... an uneasy, eerie quiet. The general raised his hand and the contingent stopped. That's when the woods around them exploded. The sound of musket fire echoed through the trees. The French and American soldiers didn't stand a chance. Most of them were hit before they could even reach for their weapons. The entire skirmish was over in a matter of minutes.

The British Troops emerged from their hiding places in the bushes and behind the rocks and trees. They walked among their fallen foes to see if any were still alive. They heard a moan coming from the fallen general, and they rushed to his side.

The British officer kneeled to the ground and raised the general's head.

With his last gasp the dying general exclaimed, "That was no bacon tree, that was a ham bush!"

THE MYSTERY BEHIND THE RED CAPE

Back in the days when ships were ships and men were men, the Navy had established training programs for their officers and men. In many respects the skills that were taught then, are very similar to the leadership skills that are taught today in the Boy Scouts. The Navy called it "Just Look" Training or JLT for short, because all of their officers were assigned a special mentor or trainer — and they were told to "just look" at everything he did.

George felt very fortunate to be assigned to a training frigate commanded by Captain Abrams who was to be his mentor. George's Navy career had been stellar to this point, and he was looking to learn the fine art of leadership before gaining a ship of his own. The year was 1813 and the United States was fighting their second war with England and could use all of the Navy officers they could garner.

For the next several weeks George was literally Captain Abrams' shadow. Every where Captain Abrams went, George went. Every thing that Captain Abrams did, George did. That's how this JLT worked. Every day the two officers would sit down and evaluate the day's proceedings. Learn and assess, learn and assess — that was the daily routine.

George vigilantly watched Captain Abrams drill his men. The Captain would show them how to raise and lower the sails... how to load, aim, and fire the cannons. George looked at Captain Abrams' techniques and admired them. Captain Abrams not only showed his men how to do these things, but he helped them. He rolled up his sleeves and he worked with them. It was no wonder that he had the respect of all of his crew, and especially of George.

After the learning phase, came the practice. Captain Abrams would shout the orders and the men would drill, drill, drill. They'd do it, and do it again, until they got it right... and then they'd do it some more. Captain Abrams knew that in time of battle their lives would depend on this. When the crew had it right, George was allowed to give the orders, and he did just fine. He had been "looking" well these past weeks.

During that evening's evaluation session, Captain Abrams told George the practice was about to come to a halt.

"This crew is ready," he said. "I'm proud of them and I'm proud of you. You're all too good to keep holed up here at shore. Time to put all of this training to work. Tomorrow we leave on patrol." George was ecstatic. This had been what he had been training for all these weeks.

Next morning the frigate pulled out of port to patrol the waters off the coast of Virginia. Captain Abrams stood on deck and barked the orders... and George was right by his side observing. The men responded without question. You could sense that they thought they were ready as well. In three days they would find out.

At about ten o'clock in the morning, the Captain and George heard the cry from the crow's nest.

"Ship to port! Ship to port! And it's British!"

Captain Abrams immediately shouted the orders.

"Turn her about," he yelled. "Battle stations! Battle Stations!" The men responded without hesitation.

Then the Captain bellowed, "Ensign, bring me my red cape." The ensign ran off, returned in two minutes, and placed a long flowing red cape across the Captain's shoulders. George thought this strange, but said nothing. The British ship was getting closer and he had other things to prepare for.

"Fire a warning shot," the Captain ordered, and within seconds the sound of a cannon was heard — and a cannonball went flying past the bow of the British ship. The British ship answered with a volley of their own. They weren't about to surrender.

The next several minutes were pure chaos as the two vessels exchanged volley after volley. Captain Abrams who was quite distinguishable with his flowing red cape, ran up and down the deck giving orders, stopping every now and then to help a wounded crewman. George watched his every move and helped where ever he could. The training had paid off. In less than an hour the British ship was in flames and sinking to the bottom of the sea. The men were jubilant and applauded the Captain.

The Captain bellowed, "Ensign, my red cape." The ensign removed the cape from the Captain's shoulders and returned it below. In the midst of the celebration George forgot to ask about this ritual. Two days later, he'd get another chance.

"British ship to starboard! British ship to starboard!" came the cry from the crow's nest.

Once again, the Captain prepared his crew for battle. Then he bellowed, "Ensign, bring me my red cape." Within minutes the ensign returned from below and placed the long flowing red cape around the Captain's shoulders. George made a mental note to ask the Captain about this strange procedure.

This British ship proved to be a more worthy opponent. After exchanging volleys of cannon fire for over an hour the two ships came dangerously close.

"Prepare to board!" the Captain shouted — and within minutes the crew was throwing grappling hooks over the side... and exchanging their cannons for pistols and swords. American's and British fought hand-to-hand. The crew could see the Captain and his distinguishable red cape in the midst of the fighting. It inspired them to fight harder. The battle was soon over and the American's were once again victorious. They tied up their British prisoners and prepared to tow the captured vessel back to port.

This being done, they once again applauded their Captain — and he they for their fine exhibition of courage and bravery. Then he bellowed, "Ensign, my red cape" and the ensign removed the cape from his shoulders and returned it below. This time George remembered.

"Captain Abrams, sir. I've noticed that each time we've gone into battle that you've called for your red cape. We never did this during training. Is it a good luck charm or something?"

The Captain laughed. "Luck has nothing to do with winning battles. The crew is trained to look to me for leadership during times of battle and I have to look like I'm in control at all times. I wear my red cape so that if I am ever wounded in battle, my men will not know. The red of the cloth will hide my blood from them, and they will not be discouraged. They will continue to fight and fight harder."

George had always admired the Captain's wisdom and now he did so even more. This was brilliant.

When they returned to shore, Captain Abrams pulled George aside and told him that his training was over. He had learned very well during JLT and his performance during the battles of the past week had proven him ready. George was to be given his own ship. He was being promoted to Captain.

"Captain George Wilcott," he thought. "Has a nice sound to it."

George received his own training vessel and a new crew — and like Captain Abrams before him he began preparing the crew. They trained, trained, trained... and drilled, drilled, drilled. After two months, they were ready and Captain George Wilcott took his US frigate out on its first patrol.

Things were pretty quiet -- but they didn't stay that way for long.

On the fifth day, George heard the cry from the crow's nest.

"Ships to starboard! Three British ships to starboard!"

George began to shout his commands, but before he could utter a word there was another cry from above.

"Straight ahead! Two British ships straight ahead!"

George thought quick. "Guess, I'd better turn to port." However before he could give the order a cry came again.

"Five British ships to port! Make that six British ships to port!"

"Only one way out."

The lookout in the crow's nest sounded off one last time, "Three British ships to the aft! We're surrounded... and they're all closing fast!"

Now what should he do? George knew that all the eyes of his crewmen were upon him. Captain Abrams had never prepared him for a situation like this... or had he?

"I've got to remain in control and not let on to my crew that this situation is hopeless," George thought.

Then he bellowed, "Ensign, my brown pants!"

PRETTY HOPELESS

Indians have for the longest time been known as the best trackers on earth. They were able to identify the tracks of almost any conceivable kind of animal. They could not only identify the animal, but they could tell you how big it was from the size of the track; how heavy it was by the deepness of the penetration; and how long ago it had been there from the freshness. They were also excellent when it came to tracking humans. They could easily distinguish Indian tracks from others by the distinctive imprints of the moccasins — and often could tell the particular tribe from the moccasin's shape.

Tracking involved more than just looking at imprints. Indians looked at the surroundings. Did anything look disturbed? Were there broken branches on any of the bushes... antler marks on any of the trees? They examined animal droppings. Animals had particular eating habits and a lot could be learned from what they ate.

Tracking was a skill that involved many of the senses. The eyes were used to check the surroundings to look for many of the signs described above. The hands were used to touch and feel objects to determine the freshness of a track or dropping. And the ears were used to listen to animal sounds. A good Indian could identify animals and birds by their distinctive calls. A really good

Indian could put his ear to the ground and tell you how far away the animal was.

Tracking was an important survival skill. Indians used it to hunt and help feed their families... and they used it to help protect their families from harm. Thus, it was a skill which was passed down from generation to generation. Fathers taught their sons, who in-turn taught their sons. The teaching began at an early age and culminated at the age of thirteen when the young brave had to prove his worthiness by tracking and hunting an animal on his own. Indians were good learners and had remarkable memories.

Actually, I once met an Indian in South Dakota who supposedly never forgot anything. I was a skeptic. I didn't believe it. I walked over to him and said, "Excuse me, but what did you have for breakfast on the morning of May 5, 1972." He looked up and without hesitating said "Eggs." "Truly amazing. Maybe it was just a guess," I thought. Then three years later when my wife and I were visiting Mount Rushmore, I saw him again. I walked over to him, raised my right hand, and greeted him like in the movies, "How." He looked at me for a second, then said, "Scrambled." Like I said -- a remarkable memory, but let's get back to tracking.

Chief Running Dog was considered one of the greatest trackers of all time by his Apache tribe. His exploits were legendary on the reservation. Once a mountain lion had been terrorizing the Apache village for months. Chief Running Dog organized a small hunting party. He chose three of his best braves and followed the trail of the lion for several days. This was no ordinary lion. Most animals only killed to eat. This animal killed for the thrill of it. On the fifth day, Chief Running Dog sensed they were getting close, but it was getting dark, so the party camped for the night. The four Indians were sitting around the fire talking when Chief Running Dog saw a pair of glowing eyes in the bushes to their right. Before the braves could even reach for their bows and arrows the mountain lion attacked. It began to maul one of the Indians. The other two braves ran in fear, but not Chief Running Dog. He quickly pulled out his knife and leaped upon the lion. It was a terrible fight. The lion kept lunging at Chief Running Dog with its sharp claws and huge white teeth. Chief Running Dog kept plunging the knife deep into the lion. In a few minutes, they both laid in a motionless heap on the ground. The other Indians pulled the body of the dead lion from on top of Chief Running Dog who, other than being scratched and covered with blood, mostly from the lion, was in good shape. The party returned to the village and Chief Running Dog received a heroes welcome.

But Chief Running Dog was getting on in age and now would face one of the biggest challenges of his life... passing his skills on to his son, Pretty Hopeless, who was fast approaching his thirteenth birthday.

This was a strange Indian name, but it stems from the circumstances of his birth. Chief Running Dog and his wife had been married for many years and had been unable to conceive a child. Every time that Chief Running Dog would talk to the tribe Medicine Man about the situation, the Medicine Man would reply, “It’s pretty hopeless.” Then, lo and behold, his wife became pregnant. They were thrilled. Unfortunately, due to her age, it was a rough child birth. Once again, the Medicine Man said the situation looked "pretty hopeless". He proved to be right. The mother died during child birth, but the Medicine Man was able to save the baby, a baby boy. Thus, Chief Running Dog named him "Pretty Hopeless".

Chief Running Dog was a highly respected Chief, and many of his fellow tribesmen and tribeswomen helped to raise his son in the best Indian traditions. Unfortunately, the general conclusion was that Pretty Hopeless was aptly named. He couldn't do anything right. It's not that he didn't try. Many times he probably tried too hard. He just couldn't get it. Even the simplest Indian tasks were a challenge. It was so bad they had to resort to putting an "L" and an "R" inside of his moccasins so he'd get them on the proper feet.

Now came the time for Chief Running Dog to teach Pretty Hopeless hunting and tracking skills. Both knew that soon he would have to prove his manhood by hunting an animal on his own. The good Chief spent many weeks teaching Pretty Hopeless how to use his bow to shoot arrows accurately. He taught him how to use his knife. They would often go for long excursions into the woods, sometimes for days at a time, where Chief Running Dog tried to teach Pretty Hopeless about tracks... sounds... and how to use his senses. They didn't have much time — Pretty Hopeless would be thirteen in three more days.

A week later Chief Running Dog declared Pretty Hopeless ready... or at least as ready as he'd ever be. He assembled the other chiefs and braves to the ceremonial area where he presented Pretty Hopeless with his own knife, bow, and a quiver full of arrows. He was instructed to go off into the woods and not return until he had killed his first animal on his own. Pretty Hopeless was a bit apprehensive... a bit scared. He didn't know if he was ready, but he couldn't embarrass his father. He headed for the woods on a trot.

He had only been gone a few minutes when an awful commotion came from the woods, not far from where Pretty Hopeless had entered. It sounded like one heck of a fight. It reminded Chief Running Dog of his scrap with the mountain lion many years ago. "This would be a record," exclaimed one of the other braves as they slowly returned to the ceremonial area. After about ten minutes there was silence. The whole tribe waited in anticipation. Then Pretty Hopeless emerged from the woods. The braves gave hoots and cheers. Unfortunately, most of them were "Boo's." In Pretty Hopeless' right hand he held his knife... and in his left hand, gingerly held by its tail, was his game — a chipmunk.

"Sorry, you'll have to do better than that," the Chief explained, as he directed Pretty Hopeless back toward the woods.

This time Pretty Hopeless was gone for hours looking for tracks and signs. He wandered down by the lake, but he didn't see any. He walked through the woods. He walked along the trails... but nothing. He was beginning to feel frustrated. He was also beginning to feel lost. He sat down and tried to remember his father's teachings — "Remain calm."

"Okay, I've got to remain calm. But then what?"

" If you ever get lost, remember the rule of three — build three fires..."

"But they didn't give me any matches!"

"...or fire three shots from your rifle."

"But they didn't give me a rifle, just this bow and arrows."

Pretty Hopeless thought for a minute. "Boy, was I stupid. This was a test and they want to see how well I can think on my own."

Quickly, he took his bow and fired three arrows into the air.

"There, now they'll know I'm lost and come looking for me. Meanwhile, I'd better get to my tracking."

Ten minutes later, Pretty Hopeless saw his first sign and what a relief. It was nailed to a tree and read "RESERVATION SIX MILES."

"At least now I know I can get back."

But Pretty Hopeless knew he couldn't go back yet. He had not yet killed his animal. He followed the trail in the other direction. In about a mile it exited the woods. He was now in the valley. His father had told him stories of the valley.

"That's where the settlers live... in their houses."

He looked... and, sure enough, on the horizon he could make out the faint image of buildings. He was about ready to turn back into the woods when he saw something strange on the ground ahead. He ran to investigate.

"Oh, my gosh, tracks!"

Pretty Hopeless was excited — but he was also afraid. In all of his training with Chief Running Dog he had never seen tracks like these. These were so big.

"Use your senses," he thought.

He used his eyes. He observed that this creature had probably threatened the settlers because the tracks headed directly toward town. He used his hands. Pretty Hopeless bent down and touched the tracks. He was confused. The tracks were hard which indicated they had been there a while... yet were warm indicating they were recent. That's when he heard the rumble in the distance. Pretty Hopeless put his ear to the ground and listened. It sounded louder than a herd of stampeding buffalos — and it was getting closer. He had to warn the town. He got up and started running.

It was late that evening and Chief Running Dog and his fellow Indians were still waiting for the return of Pretty Hopeless when they heard noise coming from the trail. Everyone thought that Pretty Hopeless had returned... but they were wrong. It was the sheriff from town — and he had bad news.

There had been an accident and Pretty Hopeless was dead.

"For some strange reason," the sheriff explained, "he was running on the railroad tracks and got hit by a train."

THE STALKER

What is anyone's worst fear? I think it's knowing that something is out there. Something you can't see but you can feel. Something you know is going to do something... but you don't know what... but it's probably not good. Something you try to avoid... but it keeps coming back. It's these kind of fears that eat at your nerves and drive you crazy. Jimmy Johnson had these kind of fears.

Jimmy Johnson was eleven years old and a pretty active child. He played Little League Baseball, Football, and was a member of the local Boy Scout Troop. By most standards he was your typical boy. Until he heard what had happened to his best friend Alfred.

One day while on his way home from baseball practice, Alfred thought he was being followed. It wasn't that he saw anyone. He just sensed it. He turned around several times, but didn't see anybody. So he walked faster. He was still a half mile from home and the sun was setting fast when he thought he heard footsteps behind him. He decided to turn into the woods and take a shortcut, this time running as fast as he could. Now he was sure he heard the sound of feet... and they were definitely coming after him.

Then Alfred heard it.

"Stop. Don't be afraid. I just want to show you

what I can do with these big purple lips and long skinny fingers!"

Alfred kept running. He had no intentions of finding out what this person... or thing... could do. He was running so fast, however, that he didn't see this root protruding from the ground. Alfred tripped, falling forward into this small clearing. As he got up, he could hear the sound of someone... or something almost upon him. He froze.

Just then the figure of a man appeared on the path and once again the figure uttered, "Don't be afraid. I just want to show you what I can do with these big purple lips and long skinny fingers!"

Alfred could see those big purple lips... and those long skinny fingers...but he wanted nothing to do with them. He turned and ran again. The man turned to run as well, but like Alfred he did not see the tree root protruding from the path and tripped.

This was just the time Alfred needed to get away. He arrived home safely, but scared and out of breath. He told his parents his story and they informed the police, but after a thorough search of the area the police found nothing... and nobody in town knew of anyone with big purple lips and long skinny fingers. The story made the local papers, but that was pretty much it.

Many of Alfred's friends said he made the whole story up and some even teased him about it... but not Jimmy. Being best friends, Jimmy and Alfred shared many secrets... and Jimmy just knew Alfred wasn't lying. He could sense the fear in Alfred's voice as he repeated the story. So Jimmy stuck up for his friend.

Jimmy thought a lot about the incident. What would he have done if someone were after him? Could he take care of himself? Why were their friends being so insensitive? Why didn't they believe Alfred? But the question that concerned him the most — what was the man going to do with those big purple lips and long skinny fingers?

Then a week later it happened. During school Jimmy found a note tucked in the front of his math book. It was made from letters which had been cut from magazines and then pasted to form a sentence. The sentence read, "I want to show you what I can do with these big purple lips and long skinny fingers." Jimmy knew this had to be a practical joke. He looked around the classroom but could see no one laughing or smiling.

"Maybe this isn't a joke," he thought.

After school he shared the letter with Alfred. He also believed it was a joke. "Must be some of our so-called friends poking fun at us again," Alfred added. Jimmy nodded, but deep down inside he wasn't so sure. They threw the note away.

They thought nothing of it until a few days later when Jimmy's phone rang. Jimmy picked up the receiver and answered.

"Hello. Johnson residence. Jimmy speaking."

There was silence on the other end.

"Hello," Jimmy repeated.

Then in a deep voice he heard "Don't be afraid. I just want to show you what I can do with these big purple lips and long skinny fingers!"

Jimmy hung up.

"Who is doing this?" he thought. "I wish they'd stop." This time Jimmy decided to tell his parents, something he now realized he should have done immediately. He told them about the teasing, the note at school, and the phone call. His parents went to the school to talk to Jimmy's teachers who in turn talked to the students.

They really weren't sure this would do anything, but to their surprise two boys came forwarded and confessed. They told how they had put the note together and had convinced one of their older brothers to make the phone call. They were sincerely sorry. They thought it would be fun.

Nobody was more relieved than Jimmy. He could now get back to being a boy without believing there was a bogey man behind every corner. And just in time too, because that coming weekend was the Troop's big campout at Darby Creek. Both he and Alfred were looking forward to getting away from town. Perhaps then they could forget about those "big purple lips and long skinny fingers!"

And so Friday came and Jimmy and Alfred joined the other Scouts for a weekend of fun at Darby Creek. They pitched their tents, laughed, joked, and completely forgot about the troubles of the past few weeks. They felt so at peace that on Saturday Jimmy, Alfred, and a few of the other Scouts decided to explore the woods around the campsite. They'd only been hiking a short distance when one of the boys noticed something to the right.

"Look! Over there! I think I see a fire. There's grey smoke." The boys went to investigate.

He was right. There in a small clearing was a makeshift shelter, a few old blankets, and a campfire which was practically all coals, probably left burning from breakfast.

"Bad practice," Alfred said. "This fire shouldn't have been left like this. It should have been completely put out." The other Scouts agreed and began to cover it with soil.

That's when they heard it. The sound of someone coming down the path. They didn't know what to do. Should they run? Should they stay?

"Why should we run?" Jimmy said. "We're only doing them a favor by putting out the fire." So they stayed.

In a few minutes the figure of a man appeared in the clearing. He wore old, tattered clothing and apparently hadn't shaved or washed for several days... but his most distinguishing features were he had big purple lips and long skinny fingers.

Alfred and Jimmy screamed.

"That's the man who chased me," Alfred yelled.

All of the Scouts ran for the woods.

"Don't be afraid. I just want to show you what I can do with these big purple lips and long skinny fingers!" yelled the man.

Scoutleaders from the nearby campsite heard the screams and responded immediately, holding the man while they went to get the authorities. He seemed rather harmless. He kept sobbing, "All I wanted to do was show them what I can do with these big purple lips and long skinny fingers."

The police came and took the man to the station where they questioned him. He was a drifter who had recently run away from a mental institution and had been camping in the woods the past few weeks because he didn't have a home. He admitted to chasing Alfred, but said he didn't mean him any harm.

" I only wanted to show him what I can do with these big purple lips and log skinny fingers!"

"And just what is it you can do?" the officer asked.

The old man smiled. Took his long skinny fingers and placed them to his big purple lips — and went bbbbbbbbbbbbb.

(With the latter the storyteller should take his index finger to his lips and vibrate them making the "bbbbbbbbb" sound.)

EXPERIENCES IN COOKING

(This story is dedicated to all Scouters who have ever served as a Patrol Advisor or helped an inexperienced patrol on a campout.)

Cooking can be a challenge for any patrol, but cooking for an unseasoned patrol can really be an experience... both for the cookers, the instructors, and the eaters. This was going to be the Beaver Patrol's first cooking experience together, since all of the boys had been in Scouting for less than two months, some having come from Webelos... others during Spring recruitment. Even the Troop Guide for this "new boy" patrol was relatively inexperienced, having joined only the year before.

Troop 474 believed in the Patrol Method so the Beaver Patrol was responsible for everything — planning the menu, buying the food, cooking the meal, and clean up. Juan Gonzales, their Troop Guide, worked with the boys at the Troop Meeting to help them plan the menu. All of the boys were enthusiastic... but too much so. None of them could agree on anything.

"That's terrible!" "I don't like that!" "Pleeeese, no onions!"

"I'm allergic to that!"

Juan was hearing it all. Finally, he turned to Tony, the newly elected patrol leader, and said, "Sort it out. You've got ten minutes," and walked over to see the Scoutmaster.

"Help!" Juan pleaded to the Scoutmaster. "These boys can't agree on anything. This is going to be a long campout."

"Just give them a chance," the Scoutmaster said encouragingly. "They've never done this before. And besides, I have decided to be your advisor for the weekend and give you a hand."

"Thanks, I'll need it," Juan responded.

The ten minutes was up and Juan walked with the Scoutmaster back to the patrol.

"There, we're done," said Tony as he handed Juan a paper containing the menu for the coming weekend. Juan looked at the Scoutmaster and acknowledged, "Maybe there is hope."

The next evening the Scouts met at Tony's house to go food shopping. The whole patrol was there to help. Tony's mom piled them into the van and took them to the food market. She offered to help, but the Scouts were insistent that they could do it themselves. Juan wasn't so sure.

"See you in an hour," she said as she drove off.

The boys got a shopping cart. Tony had the list and gave orders... as Scouts ran all over the store in search of items. On their return they put them in the cart and received a new item to retrieve from Tony. Juan just stood there supervising... or I should say yelling... mostly things like "Not enough of that!" "Too much of that!" "What are you going to use that for?" He was also doing rough cost calculations on his calculator. In forty minutes, much of which was spent returning wrong items to the shelf, they were done.

"How are we doing?" asked Tony, as Juan poked the last figures into his calculator.

"Well, according to my figures, you're about eighteen dollars over budget... but if you get rid of all the soft drinks, potato chips, cookies, and other junk food you guys have been sneaking into the cart I think you'll be okay." So they made one more trip returning stuff to the shelves and then checked out, right on time to meet Tony's mom.

Friday evening, about an hour before the time to leave, the phone rang in the home of the Scoutmaster. It was Juan. "Hello, *cough* it's me Juan *cough cough*, I'm sick *cough* and won't be able go on the *cough* campout."

"You don't sound so good. Stay home and take care of yourself."

"I hope *cough* those new boys will *cough* be okay." Juan was a good leader, always thinking of the boys in his charge.

"Don't worry. I'll take care of them myself," replied the Scoutmaster

Juan hung up the phone knowing that his new boy patrol was in good hands. The Scoutmaster would give them the guidance they needed, particularly when it came to cooking.

The Scouts met at the Troop hall and loaded all their gear into the vehicles for the three hour ride to camp. The ride was uneventful except for two *pit stops* along the way. The second one was unplanned — but Harold convinced them he really had to go.

At camp the Scouts unloaded the gear and began putting up the tents. Each patrol had their own area, complete with a fire ring for cooking and a picnic table for eating. The Scouts hurried because it was already getting dark The Scoutmaster lit a lantern and placed it on the picnic table and said, "Time for cracker barrel! What's on the menu?"

Tony checked and replied, "Crackers and cheese. What else?" He sent one of the patrol members to the truck to get the stuff. A few minutes later he returned, carrying only the crackers.

"I couldn't find the cheese."

Tony thought for a minute and said, "I know right where it is." Then after a moment's hesitation added, "At home in my refrigerator... along with the other perishables."

At this point, nobody was willing to drive six hours round trip for the needed food. The Scoutmaster wasn't happy, but mistakes happen. He told the other adults he was going into town and asked Tony for the menu. Meanwhile the new boys enjoyed their cracker barrel of crackers and crackers.

The next morning the boys arose to find that their perishables had all been restocked thanks to the Scoutmaster. It was time to build a fire and cook breakfast. Tony had the Scouts look for firewood while he tried to start the fire. The firewood gatherers were having great success... but not Tony.

"It won't light! It just won't light!"

The Scoutmaster went to see what was wrong... besides he wanted to get that fire going so he could have his morning coffee. He saw the problem right off. Tony was using wood that was too big. He had no kindling or anything... and he had no idea as to how to light it.

The Scoutmaster pulled the Scouts together and showed them how to make a fire. He started with some kindling, broke lots of fine twigs, and finally some larger twigs. Then he showed them how to light it from the bottom. It was lit in a second.

"Tony, what's for breakfast?"

"Pancakes."

"Great! Get your cooking crew over here... but first put this water on the fire while I help these boys mix the batter." After the fire building episode the Scoutmaster really needed that cup of coffee.

Tony stopped and stared quizzically at the Scoutmaster for a second. Then left the cooking area and promptly poured the water on the fire.

"Why did you do that?" the other Scouts yelled.

"Because the Scoutmaster told me to," Tony yelled back.

The Scoutmaster heard the commotion and left the picnic table to see what was going on. His last instructions were "Make sure you get out the lumps in the batter!"

He immediately sized up the situation, calmed the Scouts, and pulled Tony aside. "I meant for you to put the pot on the fire, not the water."

"Then you should have said so."

No time for arguing. The Scoutmaster helped the Scouts rebuild the fire and then returned to the picnic table.

"How's it going with the batter?"

"Great, I think we're done."

The Scoutmaster looked down.

"What are you guys making — pancake soup? How much water did you put in that?"

"I don't know," came the reply, "but there are no lumps!"

The only way they were going to serve these pancakes was with straws. Time to improvise.

"Geeeze, this maple syrup on bread isn't bad," mumbled the Scouts as they ate breakfast.

The Scoutmaster just mumbled.

After a morning of activities, came lunch — tomato soup and grilled cheese sandwiches. While Tony and a few boys started opening the cans of soup and making the sandwiches, the Scoutmaster gathered the others around.

"If you want to make your clean up easy," he said, "you need to soap the pot."

"Soap the pot?" a Scout said, looking bewildered.

"Yes. If you cover the pot with dish washing soap it will make it much easier to clean." He then went to see how lunch was coming. No problem opening the soup, but Tony could use a hand with the sandwiches.

As the Scoutmaster and Tony placed the sandwiches on the grill, the Scoutmaster noticed this film on top of the tomato soup which was cooking on the fire.

"That looks like soap!"

"Oh, it is," the boys said proudly. "We soaped the pot just like you said.

"You weren't supposed to soap the inside?"

"You didn't say that."

The Scoutmaster was frustrated. You can't eat that. We'll have to throw it away. He reached to take the pot off the fire... forgetting to use the cooking glove.

"Ouch!" He burned his fingers. The Scoutmaster ran to the picnic table to get the cooking glove. When he returned he smelled something burning.

"The sandwiches. Didn't you flip the sandwiches?"

"Nobody told me too."

Quickly, the Scoutmaster took the soup off the fire and started flipping sandwiches. The bottoms were black. The patrol had their lunch of grilled, or rather carbonized, cheese sandwiches.

In the afternoon the Scouts continued their activities. The Scoutmaster excused himself and took a long walk in the woods, explaining he needed to gain his composure. He was back for supper, more determined than ever. Supper was spaghetti — and what could go wrong with that. Nothing, because he wasn't going to allow it!

He was right there when the boys cooked the meat and added the sauce. He was there when they soaped the pot for the water. He was there when they added the spaghetti to the boiling water... and he was there every time they stirred the pot. It all went well. All that was left was draining the water and eating.

"Tony, come with me while I drain the water. It's too hot for you guys to do." "Besides," he thought to himself, "at this point there's no way I'd let you."

Draining spaghetti without a colander is a tedious process... but not hard if you know what you're doing... and the Scoutmaster knew what he was doing. He held the pot cover to the pot, this time using the cooking gloves, leaving a small opening just large enough for the water to escape. He then tilted the pot. It worked fine, but the steam from the escaping water caused his glasses to fog. By the time he was done, he couldn't see anymore. He told Tony to put on the cooking gloves and take the spaghetti over to the table.

"We're ready to eat," he exclaimed.

He was cleaning his glasses, so he didn't see it happen, but he sure did hear it. First the thud as Tony's foot hit the rock... then the sound of him and the pot of spaghetti hitting the ground. He had tripped... and tripped big time. Thank goodness he was okay, but the spaghetti was a total loss. It was on the ground... in the bushes... and up in the trees. The Scouts used their spoons to eat the spaghetti sauce for supper.

The Scoutmaster went to bed early. He had had a rough day. And to think, he still had to look forward to breakfast.

Next morning the Scouts awoke to a surprise. The Scoutmaster wanted them all to pack their gear as soon as possible because they were leaving early.

"But what about breakfast?"

"That's the surprise. We're stopping at McDonald's." Everyone was packed in record time.

It was eleven in the morning when the Scouts pulled up to the Troop hall. Juan was there to meet them. He was feeling much better. The Scoutmaster was busy unloading gear, so Juan asked Tony, "How did it go? Learn anything about cooking?"

"Yeah, I think we learned how to make a Scoutmaster stew."

HIS FATHER'S RING

Tommy Sprague was bridging from Webelos to Boy Scouts and his Cub Pack was having a big ceremony. You see, Tommy Sprague was becoming a fourth generation Boy Scout. His father, his grandfather, and his great-grandfather had all been Eagle Scouts, so needless to say this was a proud moment for his family. His mom, his dad, and his sister were all standing there to greet him as he crossed the bridge.

Scouting had always been a family affair with the Sprague's. Mr. Sprague had been an active adult ever since Tommy joined Tiger Cubs; Mrs. Sprague had been a Den Leader for two years and also worked with the Girl Scouts; and Tommy's sister was an active Girl Scout. This was a very close family. Mr. Sprague and Tommy did most everything together. They both loved fishing, camping, hiking, and, of course, Scouting.

This was about to change. Within two months of Tommy's graduation into Boy Scouts, Mr. Sprague became ill, seriously ill. The doctors weren't exactly sure what he had, but it was sapping all his strength. He was always run down. It was a real effort for Mr. Sprague to attend the Court of Honor when Tommy made his Tenderfoot, but he made it. He wouldn't have missed it for the world.

Mr. Sprague's condition continued to deteriorate. Three month's later when Tommy received his Second Class, he was bedridden and could not attend the ceremony. The Scoutmaster visited the Sprague home and made a special presentation, just for Tommy and his dad. It was really sad to see this vibrant, energetic person in such a condition.

Two weeks later, Mr. Sprague summoned Tommy to his room. He told Tommy how proud he was to have him as a son. "The greatest boy a man could ask for!" he said. They reminisced about the good times they had enjoyed camping and fishing together. Then Tommy's dad told him he was sorry it had to end so soon. He was dying.

Tommy was crying. He didn't want to believe it.

"It's true. The doctor told your mom and I yesterday, though I had sensed it for awhile. You are going to have to be strong and help take care of your mom and sister."

Tommy was still saying "No! No!"

"No, Tommy, it's true. You need to be brave because your mom is going to need you. Come here."

Tommy moved closer to the bed.

Mr. Sprague slowly reached out and took Tommy's hand and placed a ring on his finger, a small gold ring with the Scout Badge on it. "My father gave me this ring when I was your age... and now I want you to have it. I want you to stay in Scouting. I want you to get your Eagle." Tommy was still crying. He looked at the ring on his finger, gave his father a big hug, and murmured, "I will."

The next few months were very difficult for the Sprague family, but particularly for Tommy. It's very difficult to have fun when somebody in your family is sick and dying. Mr. Sprague was in the hospital and barely conscious when he received word that Tommy had earned his First Class Badge. The family sensed that he knew because a smile came to his lips. That night, he passed away in his sleep.

The entire Scout Troop came to the funeral in full uniform. Tommy had lost a father. They had lost a friend. It was very somber, yet very uplifting. Mr. Sprague had lived a good life and the Sprague's were very religious people. They knew that he was now in a better place, with no pain, and that everything the Lord does had a purpose. As the casket was laid into the ground, Tommy stood there looking at his ring, and remembering his father's request.

Tommy had to make many adjustments in his life. He was now the man of the house and had to be counted on more to help his mother. Fortunately, the family had good insurance and did not have to adjust their standard of living, but Tommy did have to become more independent. His mom had the rougher job, being both a father and a mother to the family. Tommy saw this was not easy and helped wherever he could. This required that he give up some things. One thing he did not give up was Scouting. He had a promise to fulfill.

Tommy made it to Star. It was a proud moment. His mother and sister were at the ceremony... and I'm sure his dad was too. Tommy could sense his presence.

Now Tommy was elected Patrol Leader, taking on new responsibilities in the Troop. He had seven younger boys to look after. Boys who looked to him for guidance and support. Tommy was well liked and respected by his patrol. Leadership was in his genes. Tommy became good friends with Eric, one of the boys in his patrol. Though Eric was two years younger, and occasionally had problems with Scouting, Tommy could relate to him. Eric came from a single-parent home, living with his mother and two younger sisters. They hadn't heard from their father in over six years. This didn't seem to bother Eric much since he wasn't around much before that either. Eric's mother was too busy with his sisters to help him much with Scouting. Tommy could relate and tried to pick up the slack.

Tommy worked with Eric at Troop meetings and sometimes after school at his house. It was during one of these meetings that Eric noticed Tommy's ring. Tommy told him the story behind it.

"Wow! You're father sounds like he was a real nice guy."

"He was," Tommy replied with tears swelling up in his eyes. "Sometimes I think that this ring is all that keeps me going in Scouting."

Tommy made it to Life. Once again all of his family was there to see him get it. At the same Court of Honor Eric received his First Class. Nobody was there. His mom was home taking care of his sisters, one of whom was sick. You could tell he was disappointed.

Three months later on a campout, Tommy heard someone crying in one of the tents. It was Eric.

"What's the matter," Tommy asked.

"I think I'm going to quit Scouting."

"We need to talk."

Tommy began to build a fire while Eric got dressed. It was ready by the time Eric emerged from his tent. The two friends talked.

"I can't do it," Eric said, "and nobody cares if I do."

"What do you mean," Tommy responded.

"You're going to be an Eagle some day, Tommy. You're a good Scout and a good leader. Your mom cares. Even your dad cared. He gave you that ring. Nobody cares about me. I can't do it by myself."

They stayed by the fire for almost an hour, before heading back to their tents. Tommy couldn't get to sleep. The talk with Eric had disturbed him deeply. He understood a lot about what Eric had said. When his father was alive, he had always been there for him. Even now when he felt alone, he could look at his ring and know that his father was near. Eric had never known any of these feelings. Tommy didn't sleep a wink all night.

The next morning the Scouts had breakfast and dismantled the campsite. Before they got in the cars to leave, Tommy pulled Eric aside. In a low voice, Tommy said, " I care," and he took the gold ring from his finger... his father's ring... and placed it on Eric's. "I want you to promise that you'll stay in Scouting and become an Eagle Scout."

Eric didn't know what to say. Holding back tears, he said, "I will."

On the ride home, Tommy wondered if he had done the right thing. That ring had meant so much to his father... and meant so much to him... but Eric needed it so much more. He closed his eyes. The lack of sleep the night before caught up with him — he dozed off and began to dream. He saw his father walking toward him. As he approached, Tommy tried to hide his hand. But his father, reached down and held it up. A sense of fear came over Tommy's face, but his dad just looked at the hand and smiled. "You did good, son."

"We're back," came the cry from the back seat. Tommy awoke from his sleep, somehow sensing that everything was okay. Everyone unloaded the gear and headed for home. Tommy told his mother about the ring, and though she didn't agree with his decision, Tommy was now old enough to decide for himself.

Six months later, Tommy received his Eagle. The Troop presented it at a grand ceremony. Tommy's entire family was there... and so was Eric. He was still in the Troop and was now a Star Scout. Tommy dedicated his Eagle to the memory of his father. A promise had been fulfilled. After the ceremony, Tommy made a point to find Eric.

"One promise down... one to go. Don't let the ring down." Eric looked down at the gold ring which he still wore proudly on his finger.

"I won't."

It took another eighteen months and a lot of hard work by Eric, and prodding from Tommy, but it happened. Eric earned his Eagle Badge. It, too, was presented in a big ceremony and everyone was in attendance... Tommy and his family... and even Eric's mom and sisters. She was so proud of her son's accomplishment. This time after the ceremony Eric looked for Tommy.

"Here, this belongs to you," he said, handing Tommy the ring and shaking his hand. "Thanks!"

A SCOUT IS BRAVE

Brian and Samuel were good friends, and both were Boy Scouts.

Brian joined Boy Scouts because he liked it. He came from a Scouting family and loved the outdoors. Actually he liked anything that had to do with fun and adventure. He liked trying new things and challenging himself. So Boy Scouting was a natural. Samuel, on the other hand, joined Boy Scouts because Brian was in it... and Brian was his best friend. He was more of a home-body. He more or less tolerated the outdoors. He didn't mind camping... so long as there was no swimming and no climbing. He was embarrassed that at twelve years old he couldn't swim because of his fear of water and he was scared of heights. It's actually amazing that Brian and Samuel were best of friends, they were so different. But that's life.

Brian was really looking forward to the Troop's next campout down at Bogert's Farm. Nearby Gibson's Creek had some really neat fishing. He just hoped that the weather cleared by next weekend. It had been raining cats and dogs the past few days. Samuel wasn't looking forward to the campout.

"It'd be nice to spend some time with you, but with weather like this, I'd much rather be home in my warm bed," Samuel explained to Brian.

"What's the matter, chicken?" Brian teased his friend. "Afraid to get a little wet." If Brian had a bad side, this was it. He often made fun of his friends, particularly those who didn't share his beliefs. But this is a common trait among young boys, and for the most part it doesn't bother them. But it did bother Samuel.

"I'm not a chicken. I'm a Scout just like you and Scouts are brave. I just don't know if I want to go."

Brian didn't press the issue.

Fortunately, the weather cleared and Samuel decided to attend the campout. Brian was glad because despite his many phobias, Samuel was still his best friend. The sun was shining brightly Friday evening when the Troop left for Bogert's farm. Unfortunately, when they arrived, the Scoutmaster gave the Scouts the bad news. Although it wasn't raining, the rains of the past week had taken their toll. The waters of Gibson's Creek had risen to dangerous levels and were unsafe. The campsite was on high ground and in no danger, but he had to place the creek off limits. If the Scouts wanted to go fishing, they could use the farmer's pond. The Scouts were disappointed, but there were plenty of other things to do on the farm.

Brian was *extremely* disappointed. He had really been looking forward to fishing in the creek. "How bad could it be?" he thought.

Saturday the Scouts started the day by cooking and eating breakfast... and then they worked on some advancement. Scouts divided into pairs and worked on knots, compass, and other Scouting skills. Brian and Samuel paired together as usual, but they didn't get much accomplished. Samuel tried to work on some stuff, but Brian kept talking about not being able to fish in the stream. "A real bummer!"

After lunch came the time the Scouts had been waiting for — free time. The boys could go off and explore the farm. The Scoutmaster reminded them to go in pairs... be back at four o'clock... and most importantly not to go near the creek.

Once again Brian and Samuel paired together. Brian had his fishing gear. They were laughing as they left the campsite together.

All of a sudden Samuel stopped. "Wait! The fishing pond isn't in this direction."

"I know," answered Brian. "We're going down to the creek."

"But Mr. Harris said..."

Brian cut Samuel off in mid sentence. "I know what Mr. Harris said... but the sun is shining and that's where the good fishing is." Then he added, "What's the matter, chicken?"

"No, it's just that..."

Again Brian cut him off. "Chicken? Remember Scout's are brave!"

Samuel really didn't want to go, but Brian was right 'Scouts are brave' so he relented. Both boys walked down the path toward the creek.

Before they even saw the creek, they could hear it. The rains of the past week had raised the water level by several feet, and the water was really moving fast. The boys could hear the it crashing against the rocks.

"Wow, just listen to that. We'd better turn back," said Samuel.

"Nah, let's go look at it," Brian answered, urging Samuel forward.

In a few minutes they saw it. The path went right down to the stream where a bridge made of logs led to the other side. The water, though scary, was beautiful. The boys looked at the magnificent white caps created by the water passing over the rocks.

"I think we can get a better look from the other side of the bridge," said Brian.

"I don't know. It doesn't look safe."

"What's the matter, chicken?" Without waiting for an answer, Brian started running across the bridge.

Samuel didn't want to go... but he didn't want to be left alone either. He ran closely behind.

Samuel was right. The bridge wasn't safe. It had been weakened considerably by the raging waters. It began to shake violently when the boys were half way across. It felt like it would collapse at any second. There was no time to stop and turn around. Both boys lunged for the other side, Brian dropping his fishing gear. Just as they did, the bridge collapsed and was swept downstream by the raging current.

"Wow, we just made it," said Brian. He wasn't even worried about his fishing gear. He was just glad to be alive.

Samuel could hardly speak his heart was beating so fast. When he finally got the breath to speak, he muttered sarcastically, "What now, brave guy?"

Brian looked at Samuel funny, but he had to admit his last actions were pretty stupid. "Can't worry about that now," he thought. "We've got to think about what to do next."

"Let's follow the path upstream and see if we can find a way back across the creek."

So Brian and Samuel headed upstream. The trail was very dangerous. It went right up to the creek's edge and was washed out in many places. The boys had to be very careful as they walked. Samuel was scared. This time he was not alone; Brian was scared too.

They walked for what seemed like hours along the trail looking for a crossing spot, but either the water was too treacherous or the creek too wide.

Then Brian saw it. "Look," he yelled, pointing upstream "Over there!"

Maybe twenty yards ahead was a big tree which had fallen across the creek. "I think we can make it across."

Both boys scrambled for the tree, but in their hurry forgot to pay attention to the eroded trail. It gave way beneath Brian's feet and he screamed as he tumbled toward the water. Samuel was able to grab hold of a small tree to prevent himself from falling. He felt helpless as he watched Brian. It was over in seconds, but it seemed like an eternity.

"Are you okay?" Samuel yelled to his friend.

"Yes... but I hit my foot on a rock... and I think it's broken."

"I'll come down and help."

"No, it's too dangerous. You've got to go get Mr. Harris."

"But Mr. Harris will come looking for us when he sees we're missing."

"Yes, but he won't look here. Remember we

weren't supposed to be down by the creek... and particularly this far upstream.

"But.."

Brian interrupted again. "Go get Mr. Harris!"

"But, I'm scared. I don't think I can do it by myself."

"You can do it, Samuel. Remember a Scout is brave. Go get Mr. Harris."

Samuel didn't want to leave his friend, but he knew Brian was right. Their only hope was to get Mr. Harris. The Scoutmaster would know what to do. Samuel headed for the tree, this time paying attention to the trail.

The tree was good size, about two feet in diameter... and Samuel estimated it was about twenty feet to the other side. But it was also about fifteen feet above the creek and the raging water — and height and water were two of Samuel's greatest fears. He stood there petrified. Then he thought of his injured friend and realized that he was the only hope.

He straddled the tree and began moving slowly across. He could hear the sound of the thrashing waters below him, but he tried not to look down. It took about ten minutes, but he was across. He headed for higher ground above the creek and came across a trail. He started running downstream at full trot.

Less than a half hour later, Samuel heard the screams.

"Brian! Samuel!" "Brian! Samuel!"

They were being repeated over and over. It was the Troop. They were looking for them. Samuel ran toward the noise shouting "Over here, over here!"

Mr. Harris and the scouts found Samuel and, following his directions, also found Brian. Fortunately, his foot wasn't broken -- only a sprained ankle. They got the boys safely back to camp. Samuel and Brian knew they were both in big trouble with Mr. Harris and they realized that it would probably be many months before they'd be allowed to go camping again. But they were both glad to be back and had learned some valuable lessons from their experience.

Brian learned that there is a very fine line between being brave and being stupid — and doing things just for the thrill and adventure was STUPID. Samuel learned that it's all right to be afraid. And being brave was doing things despite your fears, because you HAVE to do them, not because you WANT to.

IT HAPPENED IN THE PORTA-POTTY

This year our troop wanted to do something different for summer camp. They wanted something far out. They wanted an out-of-this-world experience. That's how they came to spend a week at Camp Venus.

One of the Assistant Scoutmasters had heard of the camp on the Internet. It was supposedly a new initiative... a privately run camp that catered to Boy Scouts. All of its counselors had Scout training and all of their program staff were registered merit badge counselors. The only difference was that the camp and the camp program had a Space theme. He presented the idea to the Troop Leader's Council and they bought it in a minute. This would definitely fill their need for "different."

The Scouts started planning for their big adventure in February. They wanted to make sure that every boy in the Troop had the opportunity to attend. Fund raising was planned and savings accounts opened for the boys. Camp Venus was more expensive than their regular Council Summer Camp, but it seemed worth it for the special program and activities which were planned. Besides they'd return to their Council camp the following summer. Everyone could hardly wait until July when the big trip was scheduled.

Finally the big week came and all of the Scouts were ready. There were eighteen Scouts and three adults planning to attend the week-long activities. They met at nine o'clock Sunday morning for the four hour ride to Camp Venus. After loading the gear into Mr. Wilson's pickup truck, they were off.

Cries of "Camp Venus, here we come!" echoed from the cars.

The Scouts stopped at noon for lunch at a roadside picnic area. You could sense the apprehension. What would Camp Venus be like? How would it be different from their Council camp which many of the Scouts had attended previously? Would it live up to all of the advance publicity? The Scouts couldn't wait.

It was about half-past one when the Scouts pulled into the parking lot, driving under the big sign which read "Welcome to Camp Venus." Those adults who were staying parked their vehicles while the other parents unloaded Scouts, said their last goodbyes, and drove off. The Senior Patrol Leader rounded up the Scouts and headed them toward the big sign reading "Check In".

The Scouts looked around as they walked.

"Cool," exclaimed Joey as he pointed toward this alien creature who was seated behind the Check In table. "The staff is really into this Camp Venus stuff."

And it appeared that he was right, as there were several other staff members nearby who were all wearing the same costume. It was really funny seeing these smooth gray faces with narrow chins, no hair, and bulging eyes around camp — funny but great! This was going to be a super week.

The Troop was assigned Campsite Pluto — all of the campsites were named after planets — and were escorted there by one of the alien staff. It wasn't far and looked like it would be centrally located for the week's activities. Actually, the campsite didn't look much different from their Council Camp. It had several two man wall tents on wooden platforms, each containing a spring bed with a thin mattress, and a cooking and eating area, including several picnic tables under a tarp. However, the one big difference was the toilet facilities. The campsite had a small wooden building with wash basins and shower facilities and a separate toilet building. The latter looked like a rocket pad with three futuristic rockets for stalls. On the door of one was a sign which read "Porta-Potty."

"Wow, look at the latrines!" exclaimed Billy. "It's super." The adults actually thought it looked a little stupid, but as long as it was functional... and the kids were happy... it was okay.

The Scouts unloaded their gear, got the campsite in shape, and proceeded to get into their bathing suits. Their alien guide then led the Troop to their obligatory health checks and swim tests. Many of the older Scouts had undergone this routine many times before at their Council Camp though it did seem that the health checks were being conducted in a lot more detail this year. They went over every detail about the Scout's health history as shown on their physical form. The boys didn't mind though, because the doctor was dressed up like an alien, and spoke his English with a distinct accent, though nobody could tell what kind.

Even one of the adults joked, " Looks like they're looking for perfect scouts this year."

After swim checks, it was back to the campsite to get ready for supper and then time to prepare for the opening campfire. "The staff said not to be late," the Senior Patrol Leader chided, "or else they'll have to vaporize us." Everyone laughed. The campfire was billed as something the Scouts would never forget so there was no problem getting the boys into uniform and ready to leave on time. The Senior Patrol Leader led the boys to the campfire amphitheater, a large futuristic setting near the lake on the other side of camp.

They made it with time to spare, and fortunately too, because it appeared that two staff members, situated at the entrance and dressed in their usual alien garb, were counting people. The Scouts took their seats, looked around at the futuristic settings, and wondered what kind of show was in store for them. Mr. Adams, an Assistant Scoutmaster, however, just looked sick. He hadn't been feeling well all day. He didn't know if he could endure the campfire... and not wanting to cause a disruption decided to excuse himself before it started and go back to camp. Rather than go back past the staff who were still counting people, he sneaked out through a hole in the high fence which was surrounding the amphitheater area.

Slowly Mr. Adams made his way along a dark path in the direction of Campsite Pluto. In the background, he heard the blare of bugles and a voice over the speaker system welcoming the Scouts to Camp Venus. "Darn," he thought, "I'd really like to see the program... but I'll feel much better if I go back to camp and get some sleep." He heard the voice of a staff member asking all of the attendees to focus on the "glowing orb". Then the woods glowed for a few seconds with this bright light that appeared to be coming from the amphitheater. "Wow," he thought, "Special effects, too." Finally, he reached his tent, collapsed on his bunk, and fell into a deep sleep.

The next morning all of the Scouts and leaders told Mr. Adams what a super campfire he had missed. The odd thing was that nobody could tell him what they liked about it except "It was great!" or "It was super!" Seemed like the campfire that nobody would forget was the campfire that nobody could remember.

"Oh, well, at least I'm glad they all had a good time."

After breakfast, the Scouts went their different ways to attend merit badge classes, go swimming, fishing, boating, and all those other things that Scouts do at camp. Finally, things were beginning to look like a normal summer camp. Everyone had a great day on Monday.

Tuesday was a little different. Mr. Adams noticed that Tommy was acting a little weird. He just didn't look his normal playful self. His eyes were kind of glared over and he showed little emotion about anything. Mr. Adams brought his concerns to the Scoutmaster but he did not see any problem. "Perhaps, the flu's coming on. Let's just wait and see."

They waited — and sure enough on Tuesday Tommy was back to his normal self, smiling and joking about everything. But today Allen wasn't looking very good. He was walking around camp like a zombie. Mr.

Adams decided to follow him around, since after yesterday he wasn't sure he would get any help from the Scoutmaster.

Allen attended all of the classes like he was supposed to... but he just sat there. He didn't participate or do anything. If people would talk to him at meal time, he'd just ignore them or say something irrelevant and move on. Finally, later that evening, around ten o'clock, Mr. Adams observed Allen going down to the latrine, the stall marked Porta-Potty. Shortly after he closed the door, it appeared the entire rocket-shaped structure was lit by this soft blue light. It only lasted a few seconds, then the door opened, and Allen emerged.

"Allen," Mr. Adams called.

Allen was startled. He turned and looked at Mr. Adams.

"Yes, Mr. Adams, do you want me?" Strange this was the first emotion that Allen had shown all day.

"Come here a second, I'd like to chat." Allen ran to see Mr. Adams who questioned him about the day's activities. Allen didn't remember much of anything. While they were talking, Mr. Adams noticed Joey emerging from the Porta-Potty stall.

Wednesday was Joey's turn for acting weird, so Mr. Adams decided to tag along with him for the day, while keeping an eye on Allen as well. He observed that Joey was in the same daze that Allen and Tommy had been in the days preceding. He also noticed that although Allen was okay today, he seemed to be a day behind in all of his badge work. It's almost as if yesterday didn't exist for Allen.

Later that evening, Mr. Adams watched from his tent and sure enough around ten o'clock Joey headed down to the Porta-Potty which shortly became filled with this soft blue light. Then he emerged his normal self. Something was wrong here at Camp Venus... but he didn't know what. Minutes later he saw Alexander heading for the Porta-Potty.

On Thursday, Alexander was a zombie. He was there... but not there. All of the other Scouts were their normal selves including Tommy, Allen, and Joey... though Joey seemed to be a day behind, having no recollection of Wednesday. Mr. Adams saw a pattern developing and that night he'd be ready for it.

That evening, Mr. Adams hid in the bushes near the rocket-shaped Porta-Potty and sure enough around ten o'clock he saw Alexander walking down the path towards the Porta-Potty. However, before Alexander could open the door and step inside, Mr. Adams pushed him aside. Quickly he opened the door, entered the Porta-Potty, and then closed the door behind him. Shortly, he was engulfed by this soft blue light. He closed his eyes.

When he opened them, he was startled. He was no longer standing in the Porta-Potty but in what looked like... like a laboratory. And standing there near him were several alien people who looked just like the Camp Venus staff members and someone who looked like David, another Troop Member.

"Welcome earthling," one of the aliens responded. "We were not expecting you. Now we will have to alter our plans. Please step out, for we must hurry." He pushed a button and David transformed into a Mr. Adams look-alike.

"Isn't drone technology grand," the alien chided.

The aliens removed Mr. Adams from the circle on the floor and replaced him with his look alike. Lights flashed and the Mr. Adams look-alike was replaced by Alexander's look-alike who was immediately placed on the shelf.

"Because of you, we had two Alexanders back on earth for a few seconds," the alien said to Mr. Adams.

"What's going on here?" Mr. Adams queried. "What have you been doing to our Scouts?"

"Please, have no fear," the alien leader answered, "We have been doing them no harm. They have absolutely no memory of any of this. We have taken every precaution. Only the most physically fit are chosen... all the better to endure the transporter."

"The transporter," Mr. Adams thought. "You mean the Porta-Potty."

"Yes," the aliens laughed, "It transports your bodies here and back. Unfortunately things must be lined up perfectly and there is only time for two transmissions a night. That's why we substitute one of our drones to take your place... to give us time for observations."

"And the staff members at Camp Venus?"

"Yes, all our people. You see we are a dying breed. Our planet has been torn apart by greed and war. We have been looking for just the right qualities to instill in our progeny... to rebuild our world... and what better qualities than the Boy Scouts -- trustworthy, loyal, friendly... so we have been observing your youth to learn about these qualities... Again, I tell you, no harm was done in any way. The only side effect that we're aware is the boys have no memory at all for the day which they're gone. It's as if they've lost a day of their lives."

"Why are you telling me?"

"Because you too will not remember when you are returned to earth."

Ten o'clock on Friday evening a soft blue light flashed in the Porta-Potty at Campsite Pluto and out emerged Mr. Adams. All of the Scouts had just returned from the Camp Venus closing campfire and although all of the Scouts knew it had been great... nobody could remember specifically why. Even Mr. Adams sensed it had been great.

On Saturday morning the Scouts packed up their gear, loaded the vehicles, and prepared to leave Camp Venus. Everyone was feeling great... except perhaps for Mr. Adams who had this strange feeling that everyone was leaving camp a day early. Everybody's expectations had been met. Camp Venus had been great... though nobody knew exactly why... and they all thought they had had their out-of-this-world experience.

I guess some more than others.

THE PRACTICAL JOKE

Many children are afraid of different things. Some are afraid of ghosts. Some are afraid of the dark. Some are afraid of snakes or bees. Some are afraid of soap and water. For Tommy, it was vampires. He really didn't know why. Must have been that first time he watched Dracula on TV.

The one thing boys learn about their deepest fears — DON'T TELL ANYONE, particularly your good friends. Unfortunately, Tommy didn't learn this lesson, and on a Boy Scout campout, blabbed his fear to some fellow Scouts after the Saturday night campfire. He might as well have posted it on a bulletin board or put it in neon lights on Broadway. Within minutes it was circulating from Scout to Scout. By Sunday every body knew. Any where Tommy went it was "Watch out for the vampires!" or "I'm going to suck your blood!" It was really starting to get to Tommy, so finally he told the Scoutmaster who put a stop to it.

Several of the Scouts were upset that Tommy had squealed on them.

"What's the matter? Can't Tommy take a little joke?" "He's a little baby." "We were just having a little fun." "I thought he was our friend."

Regardless, the Scoutmaster was upset, so all of

the Scouts apologized to Tommy. They had had their fun, but as the Scoutmaster explained it is not good to have fun at the expense of others. It was over... at least for most of the boys.

After the campout, three of Tommy's Scout friends were talking about the weekend's incident and how Tommy shouldn't have squealed. "I think he needs to be taught a lesson. Maybe he hasn't seen the end of vampires yet," said Charles.

"What do you mean?" asked Harold.

"Maybe we can scare him with a practical joke."

"I don't know," added Ben, "remember what the Scoutmaster said."

"We won't do it at Scouts. He'll never find out about it."

"Let's think about it and meet tomorrow at my house."

The next day after school, Harold, Ben and Charles met at Charles' house to make plans for the practical joke. They had lots of ideas. Kid's can be really creative when they want to be. After an hour, they had a plan.

"Let's see if I have this right," said Harold. "Charles is going to have a slumber party and invite you, I, and Tommy. Ben, you will get sick at the last minute, and tell Tommy you can't attend... but instead you will dress up like a vampire and hide in Charles' basement. We'll find some way to get Tommy to go down to the basement... and that's when Ben jumps out and scares him."

"That sounds like the plan to me," said Charles.

"I'm still not sure I like this," said Ben.

"Come on, we're just having a little fun. We'll have some laughs and then go back upstairs and party. What could go wrong? Are you in or aren't you?"

Reluctantly, Ben agreed to help.

For the next week the three boys prepared for the big event. Charles rearranged his basement and they built a small pine coffin, just big enough for Ben. One of their friends gave them an old vampire Halloween costume, complete with fangs and cape.

"This will really scare him."

"I'm sure it will," Ben added, "but aren't we taking this a bit too far. The idea was to have fun, not give Tommy a heart attack."

"Lighten up, Ben. Nothing can go wrong."

The boys set the date of the party for the following weekend — Friday night. Charles would take care of all the invitations.

This practical joke was really eating at Ben. He was confused. He didn't think it was right to play practical jokes on your friends... and Tommy was his friend. But Charles and Harold were Tommy's friends, too, and they thought it was okay. What should he do?

All four of the boys were looking forward to Friday night's slumber party. It had been a few months since they had done something like this. That's all they talked about at school. Finally the big day came. The boy's started arriving at Charles' house at eight o'clock. Tommy was the last to arrive and he was saddened to learn that Ben was sick.

"Yeah, he started puking his guts up right after school." Charles looked at Harold and they laughed. Tommy laughed too. Must be kid humor.

They were spreading their sleeping bags and pillows out on the floor when Harold noticed that Tommy was carrying a small overnight bag. "What's that?" he queried.

"Oh," replied Tommy, "that's my vampire protection kit... just in case." The boys laughed.

At about eight-thirty, Charles said, "Let's play some games."

"Good idea," said Harold.

"Tommy, why don't you go downstairs in my basement and get some. Pick what you'd like."

"Okay," said Tommy, "but I'd better take my vampire protection kit... It's kind of dark down there if I remember."

"Yeah. Maybe you'd better." Charles and Harold laughed.

Tommy took his kit, opened the door to the basement, and started down the stairs, being sure to turn on the light. Harold and Charles waited until he was out of sight and then ran for the stairs themselves. They waited by the open door at the top of the stairs in anticipation. They didn't have to wait long.

All of a sudden they heard a loud thud and a bone chilling scream from the basement below. Then came Tommy running up the stairs yelling "Vampire! Vampire! There's a vampire in your basement!"

Charles and Harold did everything they could to keep from laughing... and were about to tell Tommy the truth when Tommy spoke.

"But luckily I was prepared with my vampire protection kit."

Charles and Harold looked closer and in Tommy's hands were a mallet and a wooden stake which appeared to be covered in blood.

"Oh, no!" The two boys pushed Tommy aside and ran downstairs. There in the make shift coffin laid Ben. His vampire costume was covered in red. Charles and Harold screamed and ran from the basement. They ran right past Tommy and out the front door of the house. They had to get help. They had to find somebody they trusted. Scoutmaster Reynolds... He lived only two blocks away.

In minutes the boys returned with the Scoutmaster... returned to find Tommy and Ben sitting in the living room laughing their heads off. Ben had decided to tell Tommy about the practical joke and they came up with a prank of their own. Harold and Charles were relieved that every body was okay, but did not think the practical joke was funny. Neither did Scoutmaster Reynolds.

Mr. Reynolds sat and talked with the boys for several minutes. He explained that it was not right for the boys to plan a practical joke for Tommy... nor was it right, after Tommy had learned of the plan, for he and Ben to play their trick. Two wrongs does not make a right. They discussed the true meaning of friendship. In the end the boys admitted their wrong, shook hands, and apologized to each other and to Mr. Reynolds.

This would be their last practical joke.

THE LIGHTHOUSE AT FARLEY'S POINT

Andy and his Boy Scout Troop were really looking forward to next month's campout at Farley's Point. The property there had been purchased by the state some three years ago and, after much controversy, was recently converted into a state park with modern camping facilities. Andy's Troop was fortunate to get reservations for the first weekend the park was open. Of course, people weren't exactly banging on the doors because of the controversy.

Andy was only twelve years old and didn't understand all of the fuss. All he knew was that the park supposedly had a nice beach with lots of good fishing... and that it did. It was ideally located on the bay about ten miles from the town of Coddington. The sandy beach was such, because of the sand bars, that one could walk out into the salt water for almost a half mile before the water was over your head. And as you sat on the beach, in the distance you could see the remains of an old lighthouse on Farley's Point itself. It really looked strange because the lighthouse was not located on some rocky peninsula like you would expect, but rather at the edge of a long field near the water's edge. And it didn't look like much of a lighthouse, not like the big one located at Coddington. It was more like a big tower of stone that at one time had a light at the top of it. But it was this lighthouse which was behind the controversy.

You see, back in the early 1800's, a band of ruthless pirates led by Brian Farley crashed their pirate ship in a fierce storm. Most of the men were able to escape to shore, but the ship was a total loss. The men wanted to build a new ship to return to the sea and their pirating ways, but not Brian Farley. That fierce storm and the wreck of his ship had put a fear in him... and got him thinking.

"Why should we risk our lives at sea if we can make our victims come to us?"

Brian Farley had his men build a stone tower resembling a lighthouse in the field overlooking the water. In day light it did not look like much of a lighthouse, but at night with the dark and fog it looked no different than the lighthouse at Coddington, one of the main reference points used by seamen in this area. That was his plan. He knew that seamen sailing the area always tried to steer to the right of the Coddington lighthouse — and if they got confused and thought THIS was the Coddington lighthouse, they would sail right onto the sandbars where they would be easy targets for him and his pirates.

His plan worked. The pirates waited until the first foggy night when visibility was really bad. Then they lit the light and waited. Two hours later they saw the sails of a ship approaching.... just like they had hoped. Then they heard the sounds as the ship's bottom scraped the rocks and sand of the sandbar. The poor sailors on board did their best to escape the ship as water poured in through the hull. Fortunately, they were able to make it to shore because of the low water. Unfortunately, Brian and his pirates were waiting on the beach. After their ordeal, the seamen didn't have much fight left and soon they were all either killed or captured. At daylight, the pirates returned to the stranded ship and took everything on board back to their camp. They spent the next few weeks dismantling the ship and preparing for their next victim.

Captured seamen were given the opportunity to join the pirates... or be put to death — so needless to say Brian Farley's pirate band grew. This band of land-based pirates was just as fierce and ruthless as any who had ever sailed the seven seas. For many months ship after ship fell into their trap... and many an errant seaman was killed and buried on the nearby grounds.

Finally, rumors began to spread around Coddington about the nearby pirates. Coddington was filled with good people who worked hard for a living and they depended on the ships to bring them goods and supplies. They decided to send in an armed party to attack the pirates. They waited for a foggy evening when some thirty men, armed with pistols and swords, boarded their skiffs and headed for Farley's Point. In the distance they could see the light from the makeshift lighthouse. They took their time because surprise was of the essence. They knew the pirates would be looking to sea for big ships... and hoped they would not notice these skiffs hugging the shore. They were right. The townspeople caught the pirates by surprise — but there were many more pirates than the townspeople had expected. They were terribly outnumbered.

What ensued is what folklore is made of. The townspeople fought fiercely against the pirates, but the sheer numbers were against them. All of a sudden, just as they sensed defeat, they were joined by a virtual army of seamen from the surrounding woods, wielding clubs and knives... shrieking and screaming. In the fog it appeared that much of their clothing was tattered and the skin falling from their bones — but they fought ferociously. The pirates knew they could not defeat this army. The seamen had no fear of death... they were already dead!

When morning came, the townspeople found themselves victorious. The ground was littered with dead pirates and dead seamen... many of whom looked like they had been dead for some time. They smashed the light on top of the stone tower and returned to town. They vowed it would never burn again.

That's why nobody would ever buy the property. Everyone said it was haunted. However, that was until three years ago. The state claimed the land due to unpaid taxes and decided to build a park. They spent millions of dollars building facilities. And now Andy's Boy Scout Troop was going to camp there on its opening weekend.

The weekend came and the Scouts looked forward to lots of fun activities. The Park Ranger greeted them when they arrived and showed them to their camping area. It was the field right next to the remnants of the old lighthouse, now nothing more than a twelve foot tower of rocks. For some reason State Parks always like to place their youth groups as far away from civilization as possible. The Ranger told the boys the story about the lighthouse.

"Wow!" Andy thought.

The Scouts set up camp. It was a beautiful May night. There were a million stars in the sky and everyone could see the moon reflecting off the water. In the distance they could hear the water breaking across the rocks and they could just catch a glimpse of the sandy beach to their left. "Well, we'll see much more of that tomorrow," Andy said. And that they did.

Saturday was everything the Scouts had hoped for. The temperature was in the high 80's and the Scouts spent the day fishing and swimming. It was lots of fun. However, 'round supper time, the weather changed. The Scouts could feel the temperature drop and a dense fog started settling on the campground. What a contrast to the previous evening!

After eating and clean up the Scouts decided to have a campfire. It was almost dark anyway... and with the fog it appeared even darker. The Senior Patrol Leader had an idea. He and a few of the older Scouts took one of the Troop lanterns, carefully climbed the stone tower, and placed it on top. "There," he said "now we have a lighthouse to go with our fire." It definitely added to the atmosphere as the fog continued to roll in.

It was now totally dark. The Scouts lit their fire, sang songs, did skits, and were having a great time. All of a sudden, one of the young Scouts yelled "Look!" and pointed toward the bay. The Scouts turned and in the distance they could make out the dim outline of a ship approaching the sandbars.

"It looks like an old time ship. It has sails."

It was really eerie. The Scouts could see the ship despite the heavy fog. It seemed to have a ghostly glow to it. They gathered at the edge of the field by the lighthouse and watched.

Then they heard the sounds.

"Something's moving in the woods."

Everybody listened. The Scout was right. Everyone could hear the crackling of branches and leaves.

"Sounds like an army... and it's coming right towards us."

"There, over there!" screamed another Scout as he pointed toward the tree line where the ghostly figures of several men were now appearing. "It's the pirates!"

With that, Scouts began running every where, as more and more of these ghostly figures emerged from the woods. The figures carried pistols, swords, and clubs. Their clothes were tattered... and their faces were... They didn't have any! They were skeletons.

Andy watched from behind a big rock near the lighthouse and then he thought "I don't think they're pirates. They think we're pirates. They're the dead seamen who helped the townspeople." Andy tried to get the attention of his Scoutleaders, but they were too bust trying to round up the Scouts.

"I've got to do something fast. Pretty soon they'll be upon us." Andy thought some more. He had an idea.

He picked up a rock and threw it toward the lighthouse. It was a good throw and right on target. The lantern smashed into a million pieces and the campsite was thrust into total darkness, except for the faint glow from the abandoned campfire. Soon, Andy saw the glow of flashlights from his fellow Scouts as they regrouped near him.

"Are they gone?" the boys asked cautiously.

"Yes," Andy said. "It was the lantern. When they saw the lighthouse lit, the dead seamen thought the pirates were back. It was the lighthouse which brought them to life... and the lighthouse which returned them to their graves."

The Scouts told the Ranger about their escapade... and though nobody could prove it, the park decided to destroy the lighthouse forever anyway. The following day it was carted away, stone by stone, and replaced with a plaque.

THE SENTRY

Guard duty, or sentry duty as it was called years ago, is one of the loneliest but most important jobs of a soldier. After a long day's battle, sentries are posted around the perimeter to protect their comrades from a surprise attack by the enemy... to allow their fellow soldiers time for a good night's sleep so they will be ready to fight again in the morning. They do not have the luxury of a warm fire, a hot meal, or a dry tent. Their safety and the safety of their comrades depends on their ability not to be detected... on their vigilance.

Joshua Burke of the 27th Regiment of New Jersey Infantry had just been chosen to be a sentry for the first time and he was not looking forward to it. For three days now his Union force had been skirmishing with the Confederates around Fredericksburg, Virginia. This had been his first taste of combat and it had been vicious. At times the enemy was so close that the soldiers had to resort to hand-to-hand fighting. All of his training — which had lasted but three weeks — had not prepared him for the horrible sound of cannon fire or the clashing of sabers and bayonets. It had not prepared him to listen to the screams of the wounded or to see his comrades fall dead at his feet. Joshua Burke had seen it all and he hated it.

Joshua was assigned Sentry Post 4. It was just inside the woods looking out over the field where the fighting of the past few days had occurred. He knew that other Sentry posts were being established to his left and right, but they were spread out with no visual contact. About a half mile to his rear was the main Union force. It was dusk, and he could barely make out the dim glow of the campfires. In his mind he could picture his friends eating... or taking time to write letters home... perhaps playing a banjo or harmonica... or singing a tune. Oh, how Joshua wished he were there — but he had been there the past few nights, and now it was his turn to stand watch. He positioned himself low behind a large rock, rifle at the ready, and looked out over the field.

In the last glimpses of daylight, Joshua could make out the ravages of the days of fighting. He could still smell the burning gunpowder and the stench of death. He could see the trees that had been cut by cannon fire... the gear that been discarded and left... and the bodies of the dead who had yet to be cleared from the battlefield. One body in particular was disturbing. It was that of a Confederate calvary officer, saber drawn and still in his hand, that was lying no more than 15 yards from his position.

"Looks like he fought to the end," Joshua thought, "doing his job like a true soldier."

Darkness came and with it came the stillness of night. Joshua looked out over the battlefield from his sentry post. He listened to all of the night sounds. It's amazing how, when you're alone in the woods at night, you hear every little sound. Have you ever laid in your tent at night... and listened to the crickets... the frogs...

and other woods sounds? They always sound so much louder... so much closer. So it was for Joshua.

And every now and then Joshua thought he heard a different kind of sound... the sound of something... or someone... crawling along the ground to his front. He wanted to call out, but he couldn't give away his position... so he readied his rifle, and crouched lower behind his rock. "Probably just my mind playing tricks on me," he thought. That's what he wanted to believe, but he didn't really. Joshua was scared. He felt so alone.

As he looked out into the darkness, Joshua tried to think of pleasant thoughts to ease his fears. He thought of his wife and daughter back in New Jersey. Then his thoughts returned to that Confederate officer whose body he had seen earlier. He probably had a wife and family too... and now he lay dead. He was doing his duty just like I am. Joshua turned to look at the body in the faint moonlight.

"Oh, my goodness, the body," Joshua shrieked with horror, "it seems closer than it was before!" Again, Joshua thought his mind was playing tricks on him. He wasn't going to take any chances. Every time he scanned the battlefield, he made sure to check this Confederate corpse.

Stare at any thing long enough in the dark, and you will sense movement. This is true of any person... and was particularly true of Joshua who was stressed out, scared, and in a terrible state of mind. Several times he thought he saw the Confederate calvary officer move, albeit ever so slowly, toward his position.

Joshua Burke was so scared, he thought of running, but he knew that desertion from a sentry post was punishable by death. He wanted to shoot the body, but it was already dead — and he couldn't give away his position. So he remained there, perched behind his rock, his body trembling. His focus was now entirely on the body of the calvary officer.

His focus was still on the body an hour later when the whole night exploded with the sound of cannon fire. Joshua turned and looked at the bright flashes coming from the Confederate lines. He could hear the whizzing of the cannonballs overhead and the explosions from the woods behind him.

"The Confederates are launching a counter-attack," he thought. There was no need to warn his troops. The exploding cannonballs had already done that. He wondered if that would be all. It wasn't.

About ten minutes later, he could hear the screams of a large number of troops charging across the field, coming his way. He could see the flashes of rifle fire. To his rear he could also hear the sound of his Union comrades rushing forward to meet the onslaught. Joshua held his ground and began to return the Confederate fire, hoping reinforcements would be there soon.

What followed was one of the fiercest engagements of the battle. The woods around Joshua's position were filled with rifle fire and the clashing of sabers and bayonets as troops engaged in hand-to-hand combat. In forty-five minutes the battle was over. The Confederates returned to their position and the Union forces remained at the ready along the perimeter for the rest of the night.

In the morning the Union general, decided to retreat. He ordered his men to go forth, treat the wounded, and gather the dead. The medics were left to deal with many grisly tasks... and saw many strange things... but none as bizarre as that at Sentry Post 4. The area had been the scene of some of the worst fighting the night before and was littered with bodies, including two who had apparently died in each other's arms.

One of the bodies was a Union soldier, identified by his papers, as Joshua Burke from New Jersey. He had been run through by a Confederate saber, still grasped in the hand of a dead Confederate calvary officer. The puzzling part, however, was that from the looks of Joshua's body, he had obviously died in the fighting of the past night... whereas the Confederates body was already showing signs of decay as if he'd been dead for days.

Oh, well, the medics had wounded to tend to and more bodies to tag. They moved on.

ON PATROL FOREVER

(This story is dedicated to those Scouts and Scouters who have proudly served in time of conflict... putting to practice the ideals of the Scout Oath — Duty to God and Country.)

"Attention to Colors." The order having been given, Captain William H. Dabney, a product of the Virginia Military Institute, snapped to attention, faced the jerry-rigged flagpole, and saluted, as did every other man in Company I, 3rd Battalion, 26th Marines. The ceremony might well have been in any one of a hundred military installations around the world except for a few glaring irregularities. The parade ground was a battle-scarred hilltop to the west of Khe Sanh and the men in formation stood half submerged in trenches. Instead of crisply starched utilities, razor sharp creases, and gleaming brass, these marines sported scraggly beards, ragged trousers, and rotted helmet liner straps. The only man in the company who could play a bugle, Second Lieutenant Owen S. Matthews, lifted the pock-marked instrument to his lips and spat out a choppy version of "To the Colors" while two enlisted men raced to the RC-292 radio antenna which served as the flagpole and gingerly attached the Stars and Stripes. As the mast with its shredded banner came upright, the Marines could hear the ominous "thunk", "thunk", "thunk" to the southwest of their position which meant that the North Vietnamese 120mm mortar rounds had left their tubes. They also knew that in 21 seconds those "thunks" would be replaced by much louder, closer sounds but no one budged until Old Glory waved high over the hill.

Captain Moyers S. Shore II, USMC
from The Battle for Khe Sahn

The primary objective of the North Vietnamese TET Offensive against the South Vietnamese and their American allies in February of 1968 was designed to seize power in South Vietnam by creating a general uprising among the people and defections within the army. At the same time, they desired to seize by military action large portions of the northern two provinces lying just south of the Demilitarized Zone. Only one thing stood in its way — the Fire Support Base at Khe Sanh.

It was early April in 1968 and Khe Sanh, which had already been the scene of heavy fighting throughout the previous year, was under siege. The North Vietnamese Army was determined to capture it and clear the way for their advance into Quang Tri City and the heavily populated coastal region. The Americans, likewise, were determined to stop them. Their defense of the area would tie down large numbers of North Vietnamese troops which would otherwise be deployed elsewhere.

The marines who defended Khe Sanh had only one thing in mind — survival. They had to hold out until reinforcements arrived. They spent their days filling sand bags, digging trenches, and otherwise fortifying their positions. And they spent their nights in bunkers and foxholes watching for enemy attacks, or taking an occasional patrol into the surrounding forest to determine enemy intentions. They slept whenever they could, but normally not for any long period of time. They constantly listened for the blare of a truck horn, inconspicuously rigged to a tree, which the radioman would sound to warn of incoming enemy artillery.

Supplies were getting low. Bad weather had halted the airdrops and the daily helicopter visits. It also hindered the ability to spot enemy artillery positions and to direct air strikes. The enemy used this time to step up their attacks. The "thunk", "thunk", "thunk" of enemy mortars could be heard at all hours of the day or night followed by the sound of the horn. Marines would dive into the nearest foxhole or bunker sometimes arriving only seconds before the ensuing blasts. Sometimes it would last minutes... sometimes hours. Sometimes the artillery attacks would be followed by ground assaults. The marines did not know how much longer they could hold out.

It was shortly after one o'clock in the morning when Corporal William Fitzgerald was returning from the intelligence bunker to his sleeping place on the other side of the base. All of a sudden he heard it — the blare of the truck horn. "Incoming," he thought and instinctively dove into the nearest foxhole just feet away. Bunkers and foxholes were located all over the base, but he knew he didn't have time to go further. He was right.

The ground shook as three mortar rounds exploded on the other side of base.

"Maybe this is it," he thought, "or maybe this is just a harassment attack." The North Vietnamese were good at that. Lob in a few rounds... knowing the marines would go on alert, depriving them of much needed sleep. Two more explosions answered his question.

All of a sudden, Corporal Fitzgerald felt this heavy weight pounce on him from above. Quickly, he reached for his weapon.

"Hold on, there! It's just me. Mind if I join you?"

In the dim light from an overhead flare, the corporal could see that it was a fellow marine... and from his appearance he could see he was a relatively new guy. His face didn't exhibit much facial hair and his fatigues didn't look, well, fatigued.

"Sure, we can fit two in here. Just hope there's nobody behind you."

"Nah. Just me, PFC Benjamin Frost. I had a little trouble finding the nearest foxhole... got caught in the latrine and lost my way in the dark. Only been here a week. Came in on the last chopper, just before the weather hit."

"Yeah, I sure hope it lifts soon. I'm scheduled to rotate out. I've had enough of this place."

There were four more explosions. This time closer.

"Hey, I've only been here a week and I don't like it. I wish I were back in Baltimore... back with my family and friends."

"What a coincidence," Corporal Fitzgerald responded, "I'm from Glen Burnie. Here we are ten thousand miles away from Maryland and we meet like this."

The ground shook as another mortar round exploded.

The two marines began to talk about their high schools, swimming at Ocean City, eating crabs, the Bullets and Orioles, and anything else to keep their mind off the exploding shells. That's when PFC Frost said "Geeeze, when I was a Scout camping at Broad Creek I used to love the outdoors, walking through the woods at night... It was so peaceful. Not like this."

"So you were a Boy Scout and went to Broad Creek! Me, too! Eagle Scout, Class of '62. You know, I really miss that place. Broad Creek and Scouting are some of my best memories. I wish I were back there now."

"Yeah, me too!"

Before another word could be spoken, there was a big explosion. The foxhole had taken a direct hit from a 122mm rocket. The ground shook and there was a large fireball. Corporal Fitzgerald and PFC Frost never saw it. They were both killed instantly. At least they died with happy thoughts... thoughts about Scouting... and about Broad Creek.

The marines at Khe Sanh held out and were evacuated several weeks later. They had demonstrated courage and determination during this seventy-seven day siege. Many Americans lost their lives, but they had saved many others by buying the time necessary for the U.S. forces to regroup following TET. Their exploits will always be remembered.

Corporal Fitzgerald and PFC Frost died as heroes. Their bodies were returned to the United States for burial with full military honors. This was a tragic end to the lives of two former Scouts... or was it just the beginning.

During the summer of 1968, a Scout camping at Broad Creek Scout Reservation reported seeing two men with rifles walking in the woods near his campsite late one evening. He called to his Scoutmaster who came running, but by then the men had vanished. The Scoutmaster took the Scout to the camp Director to report the incident.

"We're they hunters?" queried the director.

"No... more like soldiers. They were wearing helmets."

"Anything else?"

The Scout could not provide any additional information. He had only seen them for a few seconds and they were several yards away. The Camp Director thanked him for the information and added it to his logs.

Over the years there have been many additional sightings involving two men described as soldiers wandering around the Broad Creek Scout Reservation. Though the descriptions varied, it was conceded that they wore helmets, flak jackets, and carried M-16 rifles. But nobody had ever had any direct contact with the soldiers and they had never done anybody any harm.

Then, in 1983, a young Scout at Broad Creek got separated during an afternoon hike. He tried to find his unit, but became disoriented in the woods and became further lost. Night was falling and he was scared. He sat down and began to cry.

"Hello! Hello!" came a cry from nearby.

The Scout looked up and saw two men carrying weapons. He began to standup and run.

"Don't be afraid. We're here to help," said one of the men.

"We'll take you back to your Scout Troop," said the other. There was something in the way the men talked and in their actions that told the Scout to trust them.

They kneeled by his side and in the light of the bright moon the Scout could make out the names Fitzgerald and Frost on their fatigue shirts. They wiped his tears, extended a hand, and motioned for him to come. The Scout took the hand and walked with the soldiers down the trail.

Less than an hour later, they heard the cries. It was the Scoutmaster and Camp Staff coming to get the lost Scout.

"There," said Corporal Fitzgerald pointing down the trail. "Now you'll be safe."

The Scout yelled.

Within minutes the Scoutmaster and the camp staff were upon the lost Scout. He turned to thank his rescuers, but they were gone, vanished without a trace. He told the whole story to his Scoutmaster and then to the Camp Director who added it to the logs. And so it has continued to this day. Two Scouts who met for the first time on the battlefields of Vietnam received their wish and continue to serve their fellow Scouts by patrolling the woods around Broad Creek... on patrol forever. Duty to God and country cannot be stopped... even by death.

GATEWAY TO HOME

Daniel was regarded by his friends as a strange boy. He wasn't much into sports and outdoor activities. He would rather stay at home, play with his computer, and other such stuff. He had an inquisitive mind and was always trying to invent things, particularly if they could get him out of work or make his life easier. He didn't have much success, but he had a lot of fun trying. So it was much to their surprise one May day when he showed up at a Troop Meeting and announced to everyone that he was joining Boy Scouts. Everybody was ready to take bets as to how long he'd last.

Daniel not only joined Boy Scouts, but he became one of the Troop's most active members — at least at Troop Meetings. After two months Daniel had managed to make every Troop Meeting... and miss both campouts. When his best friend Jonathan, who had been in the Troop for over a year, asked him about this, Daniel replied, "It's not ready."

Jonathan interpreted this to mean Daniel wasn't ready, so he didn't press the issue. Scouting is something that all boys have to experience at their own speed... and Daniel would start camping sooner or later. When it didn't happen in July or August either, Jonathan asked Daniel again.

"When are you going to go camping?"

"I think I'll be ready to try it next month," Daniel replied.

"Great," Jonathan said, once again thinking that the ***it*** referred to camping. In reality the ***it*** referred to Daniel's latest invention... something he had been working on for over a year — his virtual tent. You see, Daniel's dread of the outdoors was a lot worse than most people had realized. He really hated the thought of leaving his nice comfortable warm bed for the cold hard ground. And his computer... how could he ever be separated from his computer... like for a whole weekend? No way! That's why he didn't join Scouts the year before when Jonathan did. But Daniel wanted to try and find a way — so he started working on a virtual tent; a tent that looked like a tent on the outside but was actually a gateway back to his bedroom and all the comforts of home. He thought it would be ready a few months ago so that's why he joined the Troop, but alas, he had some technical problems which caused delays. Now it looked like next month it would be ready.

Permission slips were due at the second Troop meeting in September. Jonathan had his and, lo and behold, Daniel had his.

"Are you really going?" Jonathan kidded.

"Yeah, I'm not as ready as I'd like to be, but I'm ready to give it a try."

The Troop was going to be camping at Cripple Creek State Park where they would be spending the weekend working on Scout badges. Jonathan was really looking forward to getting away from home and working on his First Class badge. Daniel was looking forward to testing his new invention in an operational environment.

The Scouts met down at the church on Friday night. First they loaded the Troop gear from the shed to the truck and then they loaded personal gear. Daniel took special care to load his own pack and tent.

"Are you sure you have enough in there," said the Scoutmaster looking at Daniel's small pack.

"Oh, sure Mr. Wilson, I've got plenty," Daniel said with a smile. "Actually, I've got more than enough." They both laughed.

At the campsite, Daniel was very careful to make sure that he was the only person to handle his new tent. He said that it was a gift from his father and he didn't want it broken. He even refused help from Jonathan, his tent partner, in setting it up.

"It's a bit different," Daniel explained, "and it's better that I do it myself."

Jonathan stood and watched as Daniel set up the tent. He was right. It was different. From the outside it had all the appearances of a normal A-frame tent — aluminum frame with a nylon body and tarp — but the inside floor appeared to be inch thick foam... and a little pouch on the side contained what looked like a remote control.

"Oh, well," thought Jonathan, "I wonder where he's got the TV." Jonathan wasn't going to complain too loud. After all, he was going to be sleeping in that tent on that thick pad as well.

Despite the differences, the tent only took about ten minutes to set up. Then Daniel and Jonathan looked at each other for a second... and started putting their sleeping bags and packs into the tent. It would be dark in an hour or so and they wanted to be ready. After their gear was straight, they left the tent and helped the rest of the Troop prepare the campsite. Then they had a quick game, a cracker barrel, and it was time for bed. Jonathan and Daniel crawled into their tent as the bugler played taps.

"Well, time to get ready for bed," said Jonathan, "but first I need to get my flashlight from my pack."

"No need," answered Daniel as he reached for the remote in the tent pocket. He pushed a button and a row of dim lights lit at the top of the tent, sufficient to illuminate the tent.

"Wow," said Jonathan.

"Just one of my inventions," added Daniel.

Daniel proceeded to push a few more buttons and then it was off to sleep. Jonathan crawled into his sleeping bag. Daniel placed his sleeping bag on top of the foam pad and laid on top. "He's going to get cold," Jonathan thought, "but hey, then he'll learn to crawl into his sleeping bag."

Jonathan was wrong. He awoke several times during the night and Daniel never got into his sleeping bag. And when he awoke in the morning Daniel was sitting up drinking a cup of hot chocolate. "Want some?" Daniel asked. "I made you a cup, too," he said, as he handed Jonathan a mug. "How did he do that?" Jonathan thought, but the hot chocolate was too good to pursue the question.

During much of Saturday, the Scouts worked on advancement, but Daniel seemed to spend every free moment in his tent. This is not necessarily strange behavior for a Scout on his first campout, but Jonathan was concerned. He crawled into the tent and asked "Is everything okay, Daniel?" "Oh, sure, I've just been fixing things," he replied.

"Like what?" responded Jonathan looking around. "Gosh," he observed amazingly, "Daniel's pack contains nothing but tools. No clothes or anything."

"Just putting the final touches on my virtual tent invention," Daniel said, and then added, "but don't tell the others. They'll just think I'm a sissy."

Jonathan looked bedazzled. "What the heck is a virtual tent?"

"Oh, you see, my tent is my gateway to home. Whenever I crawl into my tent, I'm really passing through to another dimension back to my bedroom at home. That way I can be camping, yet still sleep in my bed, play with my computer, or do almost anything at home I want to do."

"Oh, now I understand," said Jonathan sarcastically. "You're nuts!"

"No, it's true."

"Then how come I'm not sitting in your bedroom right now?"

"Because the gateway has been adjusted for my frequency. You see everyone in the cosmos has a unique frequency... and in order to pass through the gateway it must be set to the right frequency."

"Now, I know you're nuts."

"That's why you still think I'm here in the tent... and my parent's think everything is still the same at home. Once I push the buttons, the images become fixed... and my virtual self can move between dimensions. They can't see me because my real self is here... and my virtual self moves between the tent and home. Where do you think that hot chocolate came from this morning?"

"And is that why you slept on top of your sleeping bag?"

"Right, I was actually home in my bed. Warm as toast."

Jonathan really didn't know what to believe. Daniel's story was so strange. But then, Daniel was strange.

"Please don't tell the others," Daniel again reminded Jonathan.

"Don't worry, they'd never believe me anyway."

Well, Daniel became quite the camper... or I should say virtual camper. Over the months he continuously improved his invention. Scoutmaster Wilson could never figure out how Daniel could fit all of his clothes and camping gear into his little pack. And Daniel became popular with all of the other Scouts, as well. Seemed no matter what they forgot on a campout, Daniel had it in his tent. He was voted the most resourceful boy in the Troop. Over the months Daniel thought he had worked out most of the problems with his virtual tent invention.

Then it happened. It was the Troop's October campout. Friday and Saturday were their usual activity-packed days and all of the Scouts, including Jonathan and Daniel, had a great time. Saturday night, the Scouts retired to their tents, and, as he had been doing for many months now, Daniel pushed the appropriate buttons before lying on top of his sleeping bag.

Sunday morning, Jonathan awoke to commotion around the campsite. It was early, but he could hear moving around and talking. He turned and saw Daniel still lying on top of his sleeping bag. "That's unusual," he thought, as Daniel was always one of the first ones up. "And where's my hot chocolate?" he giggled to himself. Regardless, Jonathan wanted to get up and see what was going on. He did his best to get dressed without disturbing Daniel and then he crawled out of the tent.

Mr. Wilson was near the picnic table talking to a ranger. Evidently, the ranger had received a phone call from Daniel's parents. There had been a fire in their house last night. It was pretty bad, but both of Daniel's parents had escaped... and thank God Daniel was out camping. They wanted to let the Scoutmaster and Daniel know so they wouldn't be worried if they heard about it on the news. They wanted Daniel to be assured that everyone was okay.

Jonathan ran to the tent to tell Daniel. He called — but there was no response. He entered the tent and shook Daniel — still no response. He screamed for Mr. Wilson.

The Scoutmaster and ranger rushed to the tent. Daniel's heart had stopped and he wasn't breathing. The Scoutmaster started CPR while the ranger called for an ambulance. It was there in minutes, but it was too late. Daniel was dead.

It was tragic. First his parents' narrow escape, and now this. Nobody could understand how such a healthy young boy could die like that. The doctors performed an autopsy, but this only added to the puzzle. Daniel had died of smoke inhalation in his tent. Nobody understood.

Nobody except Jonathan.

THE FACE IN THE MIRROR

"Look," said Peter to Michael, "there's someone moving into the Murphy house" as he pointed to the moving van down on the corner. "I wonder if they have any kids?" "Let's ride our bikes down and see."

"Gee," Michael replied, "Nobody has lived in that house for over a year now. Not since... Well, you know... Tommy's disappearance and his family moving away."

"Yeah, I still miss Tommy. We had a lot of fun together before he disappeared."

"I think they have some kids," Peter exclaimed excitedly, "otherwise that bike and the games they're unloading are going to be an awful waste."

And right they were, for upstairs already beginning to unload boxes into his new bedroom was Tony Chisholm, the oldest of three children in the Chisholm family. Tony was twelve years old, and to be honest, was not terribly excited about this move. He didn't like leaving all his friends and his Scout Troop back in New Jersey. He had only recently earned his Second Class... and now he didn't even know if another Scout Troop existed.

"Hi, there!"

Tony thought he heard something as he passed by the mirror on his way to putting his clothes in his dresser drawer. This mirror was the only piece of furniture which was in the house when the Chisholm's moved in, being left by the previous owners. But it looked just right for Tony's room so his parents left it.

"Anyone there," Tony called out. He looked around but saw no one.

"I'm over here."

Tony turned toward the voice. It was coming from the reflection of a boy in the mirror. At first, Tony was startled, but he finally gathered enough nerve to speak.

"Hello, I'm Tony," Tony said nervously. "And who are you?"

"I really don't remember," said the boy. "I seem to have been in a long daze before I heard you unpacking. But somehow I feel I belong here... though everything looks different."

"Tony! Tony!"

"That's my mom calling. I've got to go."

"Just one thing, Tony. Please don't tell anybody about me. I think I'm going to need your help and others will just mess it up. So promise. It's just our secret."

I promise," said Tony. "Heck, nobody would believe me anyway."

And so it was that Tony had made his first friend in the new neighborhood... even though it was just a face in the mirror. But it wasn't long before he had made a few more.

"Look," Tony's mom said as she pointed to Peter and Michael standing in the corner of the kitchen, " a few of the neighboring children have come to play. You go ahead. We can finish the unpacking later."

Tony didn't have to be told twice. When given the choice between working and playing, the latter won out every time. He went and got his bike from the mess in the garage and joined Peter and Michael for a ride around town. Later that day, Tony returned home, went to his room, and called out.

"Hello! Hello!" he yelled at his mirror, but there was no reply. He tried again before going to bed, but still no reply.

The next day Tony found that he was assigned to the same class as Peter and Michael. "Great," he thought. He had really enjoyed himself when they went bike riding together. He also found that both Peter and Michael were Boy Scouts... and they invited him to attend their next Troop Meeting that Wednesday night. Tony was thrilled.

When Wednesday came Tony could hardly wait to get into his uniform to go to his Boy Scout Meeting. He was very gingerly straightening his neckerchief when the face in the mirror appeared once again.

"So you're a Boy Scout? I think I was a Boy Scout once. Just the sight of that uniform brings back good feelings... It's all so fuzzy... like a dream."

But before Tony could respond, the face faded away once again.

The door bell rang. It was Peter and Michael. Tony joined them and all three Scouts left for the short walk to the Troop Meeting. Tony had a super time and decided to join this new Troop on the spot. Besides Peter and Michael there were several other boys from school who welcomed him to town. Looked like everything was going to work out fine.

When Tony returned home after the meeting, he told his mom and dad what a great time he had had... and then promptly ran up to his room to tell the face in the mirror.

"Hello! Hello!" he yelled, but there was no response. Disappointed, Tony went to bed.

Tony, Peter, and Michael became almost inseparable over the next several weeks. If it wasn't school, it was Scouting, or afternoon games. And as for the face in the mirror, it hadn't appeared again. It seemed like it had a consciousness of its own... only appearing when it wanted to... when it felt a need.

Then one Thursday afternoon, Tony had Peter and Michael over his house to work on homework together. They worked in Tony's room, primarily because this room had the closest access to the games for their frequent breaks. That evening, after they had left, and Tony was preparing for bed, he heard the mirror calling.

"Tony! Tony!"

"Well, it's about time," Tony said, "looking the face square in the eye." "Where have you been all these weeks?" The face in the mirror just ignored him.

"Those boys who were in your room today, who were they? They looked very familiar."

"Oh, they were my friends Peter and Michael."

"Peter and Michael. Peter and Michael. Those names give me good sensations. I think they were my friends to... but it's so foggy. I wish I could remember."

Again, before Tony could respond, the face was gone.

This was getting all too strange for Tony. He just had to tell somebody, but who? His parents would just think he was crazy. So the next day during lunch he told Peter and Michael... and it was then that they told Tony about Tommy.

"Tommy Murphy lived in your house all his life. He was our school friend and Scout friend, just like you. That is until last year," Peter said.

"Yeah, that's when he disappeared. Nobody knows how. He just vanished." Michael added.

"Some people say he was kidnapped. Others say he was murdered. Nobody really knows."

"All we do know is that his parents couldn't take it anymore and had to move away. The house was vacant for almost a year before you moved in."

"Here, I have a picture of Tommy," Peter said as he reached for his wallet. "We still miss him." He handed Tommy's fifth grade picture to Tony.

Tony started to tremble. The boy in the picture and the face in the mirror were one and the same.

"Can I borrow this?" he asked.

"Sure."

Later that evening Tony went to his room and closed the door. " Hello! Hello!" he yelled. There was no reply. He reached into his pocket and took out the picture. He held it up facing the mirror and yelled "Hello! I know who you are."

All of a sudden the face appeared.

"You're Tommy, Tommy Murphy," Tony exclaimed. "You used to live in this house. You used to be friends with Peter and Michael. You went to school with them. You were in Scouts with them. Why don't you remember? What happened?"

"I really don't remember. I get good feelings when you mention Peter and Michael... and the Scouts. But still I tremble." The face in the mirror, Tommy's face, was crying. "Something terrible must have happened. You've got to help me. Unless we find out I don't think I can ever escape this mirror."

Tony assured Tommy he would... but at this point he didn't know how. Once again the face faded away.

Tony didn't see the face for several weeks. It wasn't till the week of the Troop's campout at Virgil's Farm that he appeared. Virgil Smith owned a large tract of land near the outskirts of town, near a large lake. He often volunteered the use of his land to the Scouts who likewise enjoyed the opportunity to swim, fish, and relax near the lake's cool waters. Tony and his friends were really looking forward to it. He, Peter, and Michael met at his house to plan the menu and activities.

Later that night the face was back. "Tony! Tony!" it cried.

Tony ran to the mirror.

"This afternoon I heard you say that you were going to Virgil's Farm. When I heard that name I began to tremble. Don't go there. I'm afraid. Something terrible might happen."

"What might happen?"

"I don't know... but it's terrible. It's real fuzzy... but I can feel it."

"Well we can't change our plans... and the Scouts are really looking forward to it... and besides what am I going to tell them. My mirror told me not to go?"

"Then take me with you. Promise to take me with you."

"Huh, how can I do that?"

"Any mirror will do. I can appear in any mirror."

"Okay, I promise."

On the day of the campout Tony packed his backpack... and remembering his promise to Tommy packed his mom's makeup mirror from the bathroom. It wasn't big, but it should do the trick. He was all ready when the Scouts left for Virgil's Farm.

It was only a short ride till the Troop arrived. After all it was just on the outskirts of town. The Scouts set up camp, had a snack, and retired to their tents. Tony took his little mirror and a flashlight and told his tentmate he had to go to the bathroom.

Once out of sight, he took out the mirror and shined the flashlight on it. "Tommy! Tommy!" he yelled. Tommy's face appeared. Thank God it worked.

"I still have this sense of danger," Tommy warned. "I just don't like it. Somehow I feel that I have been here before... and it makes me tremble all over. Keep me close so that I can help you."

"Okay," Tony said as he placed the mirror back into his pocket.

On Saturday the Scouts had a great day doing all those things that Scouts love to do... fishing, swimming, boating... and occasionally working on badges. For some reason Tony was not having as much fun as the others. He kept having this feeling that someone was watching him. Several times he turned quickly to look, but he never saw anything. He mentioned his concerns to Peter and Michael but they did not sense anything wrong.

When the Scouts returned to their tents after the evening's campfire, Tony once again got his mirror and flashlight, excused himself, and headed for the woods. "Tommy! Tommy!" he yelled as he shined his light on the mirror. Tommy's face appeared in a flash.

"I don't like this. All day I have felt like someone has been watching me. What do you think?"

"I think it's true!"

The voice didn't come from the mirror. It came from the edge of the woods, barely ten feet from where Tony was standing. Tony shined his light and there stood a big man with a beard... a big man with a beard and a knife in his hand.

"That's the man...that's the man... that's the man who killed me!" came the voice from the mirror.

Tony turned and ran, but he could hear the sound of the man coming after him.

"Turn here," echoed Tommy's voice from the mirror, so Tony turned and ran. Though it was dark and his light was of little use, he was getting away... primarily because Tommy was giving directions.

Then it happened. Tony tripped and the mirror smashed against the rocks. He was now on his own... and he could hear the bearded man getting closer and closer.

At the next fork, he thought he saw a clearing in the moonlight to the right, so he headed in that direction. Twenty yards later he realized his mistake. It wasn't a clearing. It was the lake. And now there was no way out. He could hear the bearded man coming down the path.

"Get down!"

The warning came from behind... and Tony turned to see Tommy's face reflecting in the lake from the bright moon above. Tony got down near the brush on the water's edge... but he knew he could not hide there for long as the bearded man was almost upon him.

Soon the bearded man got close enough that Tony could see the glimmer of moonlight off the knife in his hand. Tommy yelled, "Run!" and Tony bolted from his hiding place. The man was startled for a moment and then turned to grab Tony, but in doing so lost his balance and fell into the lake. Tony turned and saw the man try several times to get out of the water... but he kept getting pulled back. There was obviously a struggle going on and after a few minutes the man disappeared beneath the surface. Tony ran back to camp and told his Scoutleaders who called the authorities.

In the morning the police pulled the body of a bearded man from the murky waters of the lake, right where Tony told them. He had been dead for less than ten hours... and wrapped around his legs was a skeleton which was later determined to be that of a twelve year old boy. Dental records subsequently identified the skeleton as Tommy Murphy who had disappeared over a year ago.

Tony never saw the face in the mirror again. The mystery had been solved and Tommy could now rest in peace.

THE DEVIL'S WISHING STONE

Calvin Swift was a very frugal Scout. He knew exactly what the ninth part of the Scout Law — A Scout is Thrifty — meant. He and his family did not have very much, but they were happy and did the most with what they had. So it was not unusual to see Calvin accompanying his parents to a flea market to pick up a bargain.

"I'll just look around a bit," said Calvin to his mom and dad.

"Make sure you're back at the car in an hour," answered his mom. She knew she had nothing to worry about; Calvin had always been very dependable.

Calvin casually walked around from table to table eying the merchandise. Looking was about all he could do because he didn't have much money... only a dollar seventy-eight cents to be exact. Calvin knew from experience that most of what they had at these flea markets was junk anyway, but he did enjoy looking. As he passed a table covered with cheap costume jewelry, this one amulet caught his eye. It had a deep red stone set in a gold-looking setting. Calvin stopped to examine it closer. He didn't really know why since he wasn't in the market for jewelry.

"Ah, my friend! You're interested in the Devil's Wishing Stone."

Calvin looked up to see this old man with deep burrowing eyes addressing him from behind the table. He quickly put the amulet down and started to walk away.

"Don't be afraid, my boy. That's quite an amazing stone with remarkable powers. Come let me tell you."

"Why not?" thought Calvin. "I've got another half hour to kill anyway before I have to meet mom and dad."

"Sure," he said.

The man picked up the amulet and continued, "Yes, my boy, the Devil's Wishing Stone, here, has remarkable powers. It will grant the owner three wishes, no matter what they might be. However, after that it must be returned... to find a new owner... so that more wishes can be granted."

"Hogwash," answered Calvin. "That's a lot of hogwash."

"Oh, those are its good points, son... but there's also a bad side... a real bad side. You see each time the stone is used it glows a bright red... and somebody dies."

"Now I know it's hogwash. Who would use the stone if they knew somebody would die?"

"Lot's of people... because people are dying all the time... and besides, I guarantee that whoever dies will be somebody the owner doesn't know."

This was the weirdest thing that Calvin had ever heard. This guy was real strange.

"Interesting story, Mister, but I've got to go." Calvin started walking away.

"But this amazing stone and all of it's powers can be yours..."

Calvin kept walking.

"... for only one dollar and seventy-eight cents."

Calvin stopped. That was exactly how much money he had and there was no way for the old man to know that. Maybe it was destined that he have that amulet. He returned to the table.

"If I buy the Devil's Wishing Stone, how will I return it after my three wishes?"

"Oh, that won't be necessary," said the old man, "I'll come to take it back."

"Deal," Calvin said, taking the money from his pocket and giving it to the man. He then took the stone and ran for the car. He didn't want to be late.

On the way home, Mr. Swift stopped at the store to pick up a gallon of milk and a lottery ticket. He didn't believe in gambling, but always managed to buy one lottery ticket a week... just in case. Besides, he had spent a lot less money at the flea market than he had planned.

When they got home, Mrs. Swift prepared supper, after which Calvin went to his room and Mr. Swift relaxed in his easy chair and watched TV. Calvin sat on his bed and took the Devil's Wishing Stone from his pocket and stared at it.

"Doesn't even come with instructions."

Not knowing what to do he placed the stone in his left hand, and, rubbing it with his right, said "I wish my family were rich."

All of a sudden the stone began to glow a bright red. It startled Calvin so much that he dropped it to the floor as if it were a hot potato. Then he looked around the room. There was no pile of money, no jewels.

"Hogwash!" Just like I thought. "Hogwash!"

Then came the scream, "AHHHHHHH!" It was Mr. Swift and it was coming from the living room. It was followed shortly by another scream, "OHHHHHHHH!" This time from Mrs. Swift. Calvin ran to see what was the matter, expecting the worst. He saw his mom and dad in the living room, staring at the TV, and jumping up and down yelling, "We won! We won! We won the lottery." Indeed the numbers on the screen matched the numbers on the ticket in Mr. Swift's hand. They were so happy, but not Calvin. He returned to his room and looked at the stone lying on the floor.

"If the wish came true," he thought, "then somebody must have died when the stone glowed red." He felt real bad and took the Devil's Wishing Stone and told his parents the whole story. "Hogwash," they said. The stone had nothing to do with this. It was pure coincidence. It was their time to win.

"And besides," added Mr. Swift, "if somebody did die, it was somebody we don't know."

That was not very comforting to Calvin. He placed the Devil's Wishing Stone on his dresser with plans to return it after school. The next day, however, when he got to the flea market there was no sign of the old man's table. None of the other vendors knew where he lived or even remembered him being there the previous day.

"Oh, well," Calvin thought, "it probably was just a coincidence." Calvin returned home and placed the Devil's Wishing Stone in his drawer.

He didn't think much about it until a few weeks later at his Boy Scout meeting when he was talking with his best friend Casey. It was election time and Calvin was thinking of running for Senior Patrol Leader.

"I don't think I've got much of a shot," Calvin told Casey.

"Yeah, Barry is so popular he'll get a lot more votes, but you've got to try. I really think you're the best Scout for the job." Casey tried to be encouraging.

"Wait! I have an idea. Meet me at my house tomorrow after school."

Next day Casey met Calvin at his house and they quickly went to his room and closed the door. Calvin reached into his bottom drawer, withdrew the Devil's Wishing Stone, and handed it to Casey. He proceeded to tell him the story.

"Wow! Do you think that's all true?"

"Nah, but let's have a little fun."

Before Casey could answer him, Calvin grabbed the Devil's Wishing Stone, rubbed it, and said, "I wish I was Senior Patrol Leader." Once again the stone glowed bright red in his hand.

"Now all we have to do is wait until the elections next week."

Well, the Senior Patrol Leader election was held at the next week's Troop Meeting and Calvin won in a landslide. It wasn't even close. Calvin should have been elated, but he wasn't.

"Somebody died. I killed somebody again."

"Hogwash," answered Casey. "Coincidence. You would have won anyway."

"I don't think so. We can't be sure."

"And even if it was true. Whoever died was somebody you don't know. So what's the big deal... people are dying all the time."

Again this did not make Calvin feel any better. Dying is not something that your average fourteen year old boy likes to think about. It really hit home three weeks later when he heard the news that Mr. West, the Scoutmaster, had been diagnosed with cancer. Things didn't look good. The doctors said the cancer was in its advanced stages... and they had to start treatment immediately. Mr. West had been the Scoutmaster since Calvin had joined the Troop and they were very close.

The night he heard the news Calvin laid in his bed and cried. He thought about death and dying... and how hard it was to lose somebody you love... and he thought about the Devil's Wishing Stone. If the story the old man told was true... then he wasn't very proud of himself. It wasn't right for him to make those wishes if somebody had to die... even if it would be somebody he didn't know. He wondered if there was anything he could do to make things right. Then he remembered.

"I still have one more wish... and maybe I can use it to save a life."

Calvin took out the stone, held it in his hand, and wished that Mr. West would have a full recovery. It glowed bright red and Calvin returned it to the drawer.

It was a miracle. Mr. West returned from his doctor's visit with amazing news. The doctors could no longer find any trace of cancer. It must have gone into remission. They had never seen anything like it. Everyone was ecstatic — particulary Calvin. And was he ever glad that the whole Devil's Wishing Stone incident was behind him. Or was it?

That night there was a knock on the Swift front door. Calvin opened it and his jaw dropped a foot when he saw the old man who had sold him the amulet.

"Time for me to collect the Devil's Wishing Stone. You've used all three of your wishes."

"Thank goodness," Calvin replied, "I'm glad to get rid of it. That thing is evil." He ran to his room, got the stone, and gave it to the man.

"Keep this away from my friends."

"Oh, you've no need to worry. I always make a point to give it to somebody you don't know," he replied as he walked away laughing.

NOTES